Shopping In Paris
With Mrs al-Assad
and
19 Other Short Stories

Shopping In Paris
With Mrs al-Assad
and
19 Other Short Stories

Nick Jones

Special thanks to LionFish Music for invaluable advice over the title and lyrics of *Your Song* in The Recital.

All net proceeds of sale will go to Ukrainian war relief.

ISBN: 978-1-918264-61-6

Cover design by
Tee Blake
kreativiteedesign@gmail.com

CONTENTS

1

Anarchy

FOREST Boys public boarding school (founded in 1834) has a number of 'firsts' of which it can be justly proud. It can confidently claim to be the 'birthplace' of association football; the arts-and-crafts pioneer William Morris was one of its most distinguished pupils; and the English cricket captain Nasser Hussain honed his batting skills on Forest School's lush square.

One little-recorded 'Forest first' is that it is almost certainly the only English boys boarding school which has ever offered an Austin for Breakfast. A full-sized 1929 Austin 'Chummy' saloon. In working order. And I was one of the conspirators who delivered it.

A young engineering genius named John Gillett - otherwise known as 'Gunpowder Gillett' - was the brains behind the project, onto which three of his contemporaries were (none too willingly) co-opted. The object of our mission, he explained to us over supper one evening, was to be the maroon Austin Chummy saloon owned by the school's young Biology teacher Mr Glass. In the austerity-shackled post-war years, Glass (nicknamed 'Bunny' because of animal experiments: schoolboys' nicknames were invariably cruel) was the only Forest teacher who drove a private car. And rather rashly, he always left it parked at night in front of the school gates.

The 'Gillett Plan', as he explained to his bemused co-conspirators, was to physically move the little car overnight from its parking spot by the school railings to the stage of the Dining Hall, where school breakfast was taken each morning, presided over by the Headmaster.

"And you're suggesting that we don't even start its engine to drive it round to the Dining Hall?" asked one of the quartet. John Gillett shook his head. "Nope. Far too much noise."

"So how does it get there?"

"We carry it. It's really not that heavy. Just over 700 pounds. Unladen. Six bags of cement."

"Carry it *how* exactly?"

"On two crossbars borrowed from one of the hockey pitches. They're shorter than football goal posts' crossbars." There was a long silence as our leader's calculations were digested.

I was the 'Doubting Thomas' who spoke first. "OK, John; I'll accept that four of us should be able to lift a little two-seater like the Chummy and carry it on the flat without much sweat. Just about. But the school Dining Hall is on the first floor; up a couple of dozen stone steps, with no landing."

"Twenty-one actually. I counted them this morning."

"So how would we manage it?"

"Easy. We run the 'bearer posts' down the chassis alongside the leaf springs, then lift it for horizontal movement. Until we reach the base of the stone steps."

"Then?"

"Then we change the posts round so that they are running *across* the chassis, alongside the front and rear axles. That way the car can't slip off backwards. Obviously, we'll take it one step at a time, but 15 minutes should easily be enough to get it up and inside the hall. We make a wide space between the long oak refectory tables, take its handbrake off and push it up to the base of the stage where the Headmaster always has his cooked bacon-and-egg breakfast." Gillett's explanations were always so effortless you had to believe him.

"Ever heard of *Samana Sante*?" he asked obliquely. "Held in Seville in Spain every year at Eastertime. It comprises huge timber platforms bearing religious effigies, which are moved through the adoring crowds lining the streets by men carrying them on long poles. Just like our hockey goal crossbars."

Gillett had thought of just about everything. He folded his arms and gave a rueful smile. "We can be tucked up back in bed in our dorms by midnight. I guarantee."

When John Gillett promised something, you had to take notice and respect the fellow as he was seldom wrong. He first burst onto the scene with what became known as his exploding pellets - hence his nickname. He had surreptitiously formulated miniscule pellets of gunpowder, no more than 3mm in diameter, in the school's chemistry laboratory, which would detonate on impact when thrown at a hard surface like a brick wall. More excitingly, he'd venture out at night after Lights Out, scattering his exploding pellets across the school's stone flagged passageways. The following morning, the hard leather soles of tardy masters, rushing to reach their classrooms on time, would set off a fusillade of crackers.

In the previous winter term talk had turned to a mass-disruption of the dreaded Saturday morning hymn practice, held in a cavernous and characterless space called Big School and presided over by Forest's music master and organist Mr Buncher. Poor deluded Buncher thought that by rehearsing the entire school through the following week's hymns some sort of 'polish' could be put on the tone-deaf schoolboys' outpourings.

Gillett's plan was to clear the rehearsal hall with a single deftly-ignited stink bomb, which he would assemble in the lab the evening before. The amber liquid was stored in a small glass test tube which was laid at the bottom of a large wastepaper basket in the corner of the stage. All boys (more than a hundred) were under orders to throw a crumpled item of waste paper into the basket on entering Big School. Eventually, Gillett reasoned, the weight of waste paper would fracture the glass. Aided by a couple of discarded hymnals, the plan worked perfectly. Big Hall was deemed unusable for the rest of the term due to the lingering 'bad egg' odour and there were no more Saturday morning hymn practices.

Wearing dark tracksuits, our quartet rendezvoused in the shadows of a wall near the parked Chummy. Gillett arrived wearing a black balaclava with his face blacked with smudges of burnt cork. Over his shoulder he was carrying the two bearer poles which were passed under the car's chassis and our team gently took the little car's strain. He was right, of course: a quarter-share of 730lbs was a doddle.

We nervously crunched down the drive in the direction of the school's gaunt Victorian Dining Hall, said to have been designed by the Gothic Revival architect William Butterfield. John had thoughtfully chocked its double entrance doors open, so we didn't even have to break pace before arriving at the bottom of the stone steps. For 'the ascent' the bearer poles were silently swapped round and we looked up at the opened doors to the great Dining Hall, 21 stone steps above.

"One last push to the summit, lads," our leader encouraged, echoing the words of another school hero - Edward Atkinson - who went with Scott to the Antarctic.

But halfway up the Chummy had other ideas and began sliding along the bearer poles. One-handed, John Gillett corrected the car's slide and nodded for us not to pause or lower our load.

Once inside the echoing hall we'd been instructed not to talk, lest echoes of our voices might be 'broadcast' across the school quadrangle through the hall's long stained glass windows. With its handbrake released, all that was left was to push the little Austin up the base of the stage between the long dining tables. As John had promised, we were back in our beds by midnight.

The atmosphere inside the hall at breakfast-time was electric. All eyes were on the stage, anticipating the arrival of the Head. Masters sat glumly on the top table, silently picking at their food. An open-mouthed Headmaster walked to the edge of the raised platform, the ends of his gown tucked into his bent arms. The maids all laid down their serving spoons and you could have heard a pin drop.

"Stand up any boy who knows anything about… about THIS!" he gestured dramatically at the car. Slennett (an accomplished prankster) got the bench he was sitting on to make a grinding sound, as if someone was rising to confess. Heads swivelled, but nobody stood up. This was followed a deafening cacophony of copycat bench-grinding sounds. But no-one confessed to the crime.

By mid-morning the impasse was broken when a handwritten note appeared on the school noticeboard, in the Headmaster's distinctive hand.

'If the perpetrators of the incident at Breakfast this morning, concerning the motorcar owned by Mr Glass, will return it overnight – undamaged – to its rightful parking place by the school gates, he has assured me that no further action will be taken.' H. Miller. Headmaster.

Post-war Britain's 'take' on anarchy was a considerably watered-down version of mainland Europe's. While youths in France and Germany were honing their skills at setting fire to parked cars, the most rabid public comment you were likely to encounter would be one of the many 'George Davis Is Innocent' slogans painted on a wall. Forest School's subversive undercover 'car heist' wouldn't even have registered on the anarchy Richter scale.

The leading official political protest group of the day – the Anti-Nuclear War Campaign (Greenpeace of the 1950s) -- focussed its attention on peaceful Eastertime marches to

Greenham Common in Berkshire, frequently attended by a duffle-coated Michael Foot MP.

'Alt' literature and drama included Joe Orton's *Entertaining Mr Sloane* and leading pacifist playwright Harold Pinter's *The Caretaker*. Orton and his partner Kenneth Halliwell tried to enliven some of the novels they'd borrowed from their local library with marginalised sketches and comments, but the London Borough of Islington (LBI) was not amused.

They each received six-month prison sentences. Ironically, LBI today proudly includes these 'defaced' library books in its museum.

The best the cinema could produce was Lindsay Anderson's *If...* and Stanley Kubrick's *Dr Strangelove*. Captain Peter Barnard was the school's senior French teacher and, by dint of his war service, was in charge of the school's Combined Cadet Force. It was his flat-footed marching at the head of the CCF parade every Thursday which had earned him the soubriquet 'Penguin'. He was also a fanatical cinemagoer and, single-handed, had set up the Forest School Cinema Society. I was co-opted as his 'reel changer', humping great spools of 35mm film to the solitary projector every 20 minutes. Classics that I witnessed included *The Wages of Fear*, starring Vyes Montand, and Pontecorvo's *The Battle of Algiers*. Both ticked the 'anarchy box'.

Cartoonist Ronald Searle's much-loved St Trinian's also made it to the screen. Hard to believe that the anarchic bunch of schoolgirls were first formed in the artist's mind when he was working on the notorious Burma 'Death Railway' at the end of WWII. Searle made it safely back to Blighty, before retiring to the South of France, where he died at the age of 91.

At Forest School, John Harnack's 'alt' credentials were impressive. He was an excellent cricketer and footballer and a considerate coach in both sports. His goal-scoring prowess from penalties was unrivalled. He was a fair-minded dormitory monitor and prefect who had little time for the corporal punishment that senior boys were expected to inflict on their juniors. And he had an absolutely prodigious memory for seemingly useless information about local bus route numbers and depot locations.

After 'lights out' in his dormitory on Friday nights it was traditional to make a collection for fish and chips, which one chosen boy was sent out to purchase on his bicycle (with a dark-coloured tracksuit covering his pyjamas).

Avoiding detection by late-night prowling masters, his destination was the legendary Fish Harry's Bar. It was deemed 'legendary' solely because the original signwriter who had fixed the lettering to the shop's green glass facia had used larger letters for the owner's name in the centre. We pedantic schoolboys deemed this to read: Fish Harry's, which it still is to this day.

On this particularly chilly autumn night it was my bad luck to draw the short straw. "Right Jones: 11 battered cod-and-chips and 4 wallies. You've got half-an-hour to get to Fish Harry's and back before they're cold. Look out for the 168 trolleybus from The Waterworks at the Whipps Cross junction – they never give way to cyclists!" Harnack's final warning ("and watch out for Penguin") was ringing in my ears as I negotiated the attic stairs.

Fish Harry's was a classic 1930's cafeteria: gleaming chrome fish and chip fryers, with ketchup and vinegar bottles on its spotless green plaid melamine tables. At half-past-eight on a Friday night it was invariably empty. Recalling my penchant for stars of the silver screen, Harry had thoughtfully set aside a copy of *Film Weekly*, the front cover of which featured a glorious sepia image of Gina Lollobrigida. "I should stick her in your saddlebag, lad!" he advised, wrapping our order in the *News of the World*.

The return 'leg' was completed in record time. The Headmaster's house was in darkness and it would be another hour before Penguin and the other masters would be rolling slowly back to base from the local pub! No-one ever begrudged going on these Friday night sorties: somehow, the subversiveness made the cod taste better! I never did discover what George Davis was innocent of.

2

The Enclave

HENRY Brocklebank had been told by his GP that he had 'Early Parkinson's, a diagnosis he had always found rather amusing: not signalling forgetfulness, but a craving for repeats – at an early hour in the evening – of the BBC's accomplished interviewer.

He sat down to make a list of achievable targets that would ease the burden for a solitary, comfortably-off bachelor approaching retirement age. Move abroad, taking his 'nest egg' with him? Cuba was the only destination where he had always hankered to resettle. Whatever one thought about its perilous economy – held afloat by reconditioned vintage American limousines and Cuba Libre cocktails – one certainly couldn't fault their national health service.

But the eventual location of his final domicile was to be much closer to home. Within a stone's throw of Harrods (for food) and the Victoria & Albert Museum (for cultural sustenance). And let's not forget the magnificent Brompton Oratory, for his weekly worship.

He'd happened upon a minuscule Regency jewel after an evening members-only reception at the museum: a neat little cluster of around 20 stuccoed town houses, facing each other across a traffic-free cul-de-sac, not 100 metres from the Oratory.

Henry's excited enquiries the following day revealed that the unexpired six-year-term of a 99-year lease on one of the houses was for sale! Six years, he decided, would just see him out nicely.

The move from the Cotswolds, where he had become increasingly overwhelmed by what he described as 'The Clarkson Factor', was almost effortless. His 'Enclave' – as he referred to it in his Change of Address cards to family members – was tailor-made for his modest needs and furniture.

Most of his neighbours seemed to be foreign. The only accents he didn't pick up from passers-by were American and Australian. All the neighbours - African, Asian, Filipino, Mexican - were domestics who worked in large residences elsewhere in Knightsbridge. Since the fall of Kabul there had also been some Afghan arrivals. The houses had no gardens, though most sported window boxes. Perhaps the one 'downside' was that sunlight in Henry's little Enclave was severely restricted. The only time he ever heard a motor-powered engine was from a fast-food delivery scooter.

He had been living in The Enclave for just over a month and had even started a nodding acquaintance with some of the cheerful Filipinos who flip-flopped past each morning as he was watering the window boxes which flanked his entrance.

While he was taking his first morning espresso, there was a ring at the door. Still only clad in a silk dressing gown, he opened it to be greeted by a tall middle-aged lady in a brown tailored Barbour trench coat, with a wheeled overnight case at her feet. She obviously took him to be the butler who had got up late.

"Is Lady Ursula not at home?" she asked, leaning nonchalantly on a shooting stick which carried the unmistakable outline of a green-and-gold Cheltenham Gold Cup Members Enclosure badge.

"I know of no Lady Ursula, I'm afraid. This is Number 12, madam," he answered in a faultless impersonation of Anthony Hopkins' butler in *The Remains of the Day*.

"Yes, yes; I can see that!" the caller replied tetchily. "So where *is* Lady Ursula d'Arcy then?"

"If you are referring to the former occupant, madam, she moved more than six weeks ago. But left no forwarding address."

"But I wrote and told her I was coming! I'm on my way home and was intending to spend the night."

"Then I expect the Post Office has redirected your letter. Perhaps you'd better step inside." He led the way into the front parlour – the only room, at that point, which was fully furnished.

She took a seat on the end of the chaise longue and looked around suspiciously. "And where's the Empire-style Otterman?"

"The house was completely unfurnished when I moved in. May I offer you anything to drink?"

"A cup of tea would be most acceptable," she said with a smile as he disappeared into the kitchen, leaving her to study a copy of *Country Life*.

He was relieved that his hastily-brewed pot of Harrod's Lapsang Souchong seemed to pass muster. "I'm Henry, by the way. So where exactly is the 'home' to which you must return?" he asked.

"Antibes."

"I see. And how are you travelling?"

"*Wagons-Lits*. From Victoria."

"Not Eurostar from King's Cross?"

She shook her head vigorously. "Certainly not! Full of football fans and noisy children. And the food's atrocious. On the Victoria route you can enjoy a beautifully-served dinner while admiring the outskirts of Paris. Even see the Eiffel Tower illuminated if you're lucky. Could I trouble you for another cup of that excellent tea?" She gave him a sweet smile as she offered her cup. "Please call me Gilie."

Was it the Harrod's tea, or the tranquillity of his parlour, which had begun to defrost his unexpected visitor, he mused. Gilie told her host that she and Ursula were both Guild CLC – a reference to the Alumni Association of Cheltenham Ladies College.

"And at what time does your train leave from Victoria?" he asked.

"3.30 pm, but with a 30-minute check-in stipulation. None of that two-hour fooling around nonsense at King's Cross."

Though he had barely had the time while the Chinese tea infused to consider the options, he stumbled recklessly into the unknown. "You are very welcome to spend the night here if you wish. My guest room is all made up and it even has an en-suite shower room." Henry Brocklebank paused to check her reaction before concluding, with an innocent smile: "And in the morning I could ring for a taxi to pick you up at, say, two o'clock to take you to Victoria?"

She put down her copy of *Country Life*. "That is extremely charming of you, Henry. I should be happy to accept your offer." Handing him her cup, she gave a lovely smile. "Let's go and see my room, shall we?"

Gilie seemed well pleased with her unexpected overnight accommodation. As she unpacked some toiletries she confessed: "I'm so sorry for exploding earlier on your doorstep. The fact is, I lost my shirt at Cheltenham and was then kept up half the night by the Irish celebrating."

"Think no more of it." Henry turned on the landing and called back through the opened doorway: "I'll just go downstairs and wash up. You can take a nap. Would you fancy a pizza later?"

"Rather!"

An Italian domestic neighbour had put him onto Knightsbridge's *La Scala* pizzeria. Its pizzas were cooked in a traditional egg-shaped clay baking oven and the background piped music was always Puccini. Tonight it was full-volume *Tosca*. Rested and now fortified by two glasses of Prosecco, Gilie gave the evening full marks and insisted on paying. From her handbag she produced a veritable concertina of credit cards: Amex, Coutts, Visa.

As the couple negotiated their way back to The Enclave she took his arm – a reasonably sound indicator that she had made up her mind about the sleeping arrangements, Henry decided.

Arriving at his front doorstep she squeezed his arm playfully: "And Henry, do please stop talking like Anthony Hopkins, darling!"

3

Car Boot Sale

THE welcoming red and green banner strung across the gated entrance to Studland Park read: 'Macmillan Nurses Annual Car Boot Sale. To be opened at 12 noon by Sir Roy Strong. Charity cricket match starts at 2.30 pm.'

With her daughter Felicity seated beside her, Tracey cautiously navigated her little hatch-back up the incline under the stately oaks, pulling up beside a silver Volvo Estate, whose owner was setting out his stall of antiques and bric-a-brac on a trestle table, with the display's centrepiece being a handsome Victorian carriage clock. It was flanked by some silver Mappin & Webb napkin rings.

In contrast, Tracey's wares this miserable Saturday were pretty minimal: a box of Dinkey cars (all paint-chipped), five Rupert Annuals, two 'Royal' tea towels and a collection of unmarked Clarice Cliff cups and saucers, and a mint condition copy of Sir Roy Strong's *Illustrated History of the Making of Laskett Gardens,* a labour of love which had taken the art expert more than 40 years. She strolled across to the Volvo and cast her eye over the dealer's extensive display.

"So how much are you hoping to get for that little clock?" she enquired nonchalantly.

"£100. A bargain. You try finding one of them on eBay for a ton, lady! Lovely movement too."

The dealer followed Tracey back to her hatchback to cast a disparaging eye over what little she had to offer. He picked up one of the scarlet and yellow Art Deco cups, turned it over to examine the maker's mark and shook his head.

"And I shouldn't set too much store by them Clarice Cliff cups and saucers, if I was you darling."

"Oh really, why's that?"

"Made in China, they are."

"China?"

"Would I lie to you? They turn out enough replicas like them to sink the *Titanic*!" The cockney dealer's brash overconfident manner reminded Tracey of the TV *Masterchef* food presenter Gregg Wallace.

"So, what's your best price - trader-to-trader - for that little carriage clock?" Tracey asked coyly.

He placed the cup back carefully in the box. "A ton, like I said." He wasn't budging.

"I'll think about it," she said cautiously, slipping the Roy Strong book into her macintosh pocket. Then telling her daughter to keep watch over their few belongings, she headed for the entrance gates. She easily caught up with the old historian, who was seated in an electric wheelchair surrounded by his fans, sheltering under a tree beside the Gate House. He happily agreed to sign her copy of his book. Groundsmen were putting the finishing touches to the pitch for the afternoon's charity match.

On her return Tracey found her daughter engrossed in the adventures of Rupert Bear with a boy, who she was introduced to as Miles. "Any buyers?"

"No Mum. But a lady who wants the red and gold William and Kate tea towel is going to call back. I promised we wouldn't sell it before she returns. How much shall I tell her?"

"Tell her we'll throw in the Prince Andrew and Fergie one for a fiver." It was a part of Tracey's 'Royal Tea Towel Collection' she would be glad to see the back of. Felicity and Miles resumed their Rupert reading in the back of Tracey's car.

It had started to drizzle with rain and already a chorus of slamming boot lids could be heard echoing across the grounds as traders decided to call it a day. Propped up against the Ford's rear wing were two handsome croquet mallets. "What's with the mallets, darling?" Tracey enquired.

"They're Miles' Mum's. He wants to show me how to play croquet."

Gregg Wallace's *doppelgänger* swaggered over, wearing his leather coin satchel like a codpiece. "Reckon I'll make a move too," he moaned, glancing up at the dark brooding sky. Tracey hadn't seen him sell a single item. Picking up Roy Strong's garden history, he spotted its freshly-autographed cover page. "Smart move, missus," he observed smugly as he handed it back.

"Thought any more about the old Vicy ticker?" Tracey gave him her best beatific smile - the one she reserved for shoppers whose overloaded plastic carrier bags shed their handles at her checkout. "I'll give you £75. But not a penny more." She had picked up quite a few 'haggling' tips from the long-running BBC series *Bargain Hunters*.

"Make it four-score?"

She pursed her lips and slowly shook her head, just as the tea towel purchaser hove into sight. Tracey nodded to Felicity, who concluded the sale by popping the two towels into a paper bag, then her mother swung the little Ford's hatchback door shut as a final gesture of defiance. The fellow trader raised his palms in mock-surrender. "All right lady. £75. So long as it's cash!" At least he had the good grace to lower the little clock into a tissue-lined cardboard box, exchanging it for the notes she proffered. She omitted to conclude the deal with the traditional *Bargain Hunters* handshake.

As they reached the gates to Studland Park Felicity waved to Miles, who was standing with his mother beside a sleek SUV, nonchalantly leaning on one of the croquet mallets. In his knee-length khaki shorts he looked older than his 11 years. Tracey reflected on the grim news that next term this innocent youngster was due to start school at Harrow. He coyly waved back.

"Hey, why not invite Miles over for lunch tomorrow?" her mother suggested, stopping the car. "And if it's fine he can show you how to play croquet." The invitation was duly delivered and enthusiastically accepted. Felicity was thrilled.

"Don't forget I'm on my checkout until one o'clock tomorrow, so you'll have to cook."

"Cook what?"

Nosing neatly into a slow-moving convoy headed towards the city, Tracey suggested: "How about bubble-and-squeak fritters, grilled plum tomatoes in herbs and – your favourite – scrambled egg? I'm sure you could manage that *and* read Rupert with your new boyfriend!"

Holding it by its top handle, Tracey's daughter gingerly withdrew the little Victorian carriage clock from its box. "Hey Mum – did you see that the handle is in the shape of the letter 'W'?"

"Yes, I did! But I certainly wasn't going to tell that reptile that our surname is Webster!"

4

Shopping in Paris with Mrs al-Assad

"SO how long has she been in there now?" the older man asked his Welsh companion, as they sat forlornly in the window of a small French café tucked away behind the Arc de Triomphe.

His partner checked his watch. "Just over an hour."

"Flamin' Ada. All that time to buy a handbag!"

"*Mae amynedd yn rhinweddš.*"

"Come again?"

"Patience is a virtue, boyo. Like sitting up a tree in the pouring rain in the Brecon Beacons, waiting for 'the enemy' to attack. Remember our first exercise after we joined?"

"Don't remind me."

As they gazed out of the café window the two men reminisced about working in The Regiment. Both seemed deeply disdainful of its present-day image. "What d'you suppose Stirling would think of it all today?" asked Aled. "Especially that expensive BBC serial *SAS: Rogue Heroes* on telly last Christmas?"

"I dread to think. Probably turning in his grave. Aye-up, here come our coffees!"

A petite young waitress approached their table, deftly delivered their two coffees and *mille-feuilles* and left with a smile. They tucked into the iced pastries.

"So when did you get back from Columbia?"

"Last week."

"How was it?"

"Profitable. Boring but profitable. If you like acting as an armed chauffeur to a Bogotá banking director who never addresses half-a-dozen words to you all day. What about you?"

"Nothing." The older man glanced across the road at the discreet façade of the Louis Vuitton shop. "This is the first decent assignment I've had since I left The Regiment."

The Welshman sipped his cappuccino. "Who's the client?"

The Englishman smiled enigmatically. "Let's call him 'Millbank Man' shall we?"

"Fine by me. So what's he want – this Millbank Man?"

"Discreet round-the-clock surveillance of the party who's currently in that shop opposite."

"And the name of the party?"

"Mrs Asma al-Assad."

"Late of Damascus, Syria?"

"The same. And presently exiled with her husband Bashar in a penthouse apartment in the Kremlin."

"Didn't I read somewhere that she wants a divorce?"

"Correct. Which Millbank Man says is probably why Putin has agreed to let her come to Paris for a few days of retail therapy. Ferried around in the embassy's limo."

The Englishman had barely finished the sentence when a shiny black Mercedes with tinted windows, bearing a Diplomatic Corps plate, slid to a halt outside the Vuitton premises. The two observers looked at each other without commenting. Moments later a smartly-dressed woman wearing a pale caramel-coloured wool coat appeared, empty-handed. The uniformed chauffeur quickly climbed out and ushered his passenger into the rear.

Garry whispered to his partner: "Hmm. No purchases. Either she didn't find anything to her liking or – more likely – she's ordered a bespoke item to be specially made. Which will either be delivered, or the Embassy car will have to come and collect."

"So, what now?" asked the Welshman.

Garry paused after emptying his coffee cup. "My scooter's parked outside, so I'll tail them then call you from their next stopping point," adding glumly "which I suppose means more shopping."

He picked up his scarf and gloves and left to hastily mount his electric scooter and head off after the Merc. The Welshman took out his mobile phone, switched it on and placed it on the table. He also signalled to the waitress to bring the bill.

"Aled? Can you get yourself down to the Musée d'Orsay by taxi - quick as you like? The driver will know it."

"Musée d'Orsay?"

"Yup. It's a huge art museum. On the Left Bank."

Lunchtime crowds were converging on one of the French capital's most popular tourist attractions and long queues were forming. Garry had already bought their admission tickets and they slipped inside the cavernous space. Aled gazed in wonder at the curved glass fenestration of the huge vaulted roof, which ran from end to end of the building. "Strewth it's just like the inside of King's Cross Station!"

"Well it was a bloody train station, you Welsh wally!"

"So where d'you suggest we look first for her? And are we to make contact or just shadow her?"

"Let's play that one by ear, shall we? As to where — we'll keep in touch by phone. I'll go up to fashion accessories; why don't you take a look in the furniture gallery?"

"Wilco."

Garry drew a blank; but Aled had soon spotted their 'mark' closely examining a rare walnut-veneered 1930's English bedroom suite by Heals. Recklessly throwing all caution to the wind the Welshman addressed the wife of the exiled President of Syria.

"Lovely innit? Walnut. My Mam and Dad 'ad one like this when we lived in Cardiff." As a spontaneous conversational opener, it was clearly a winner, as Asma gave him a big smile. "And are you from Cardiff?" she asked in perfect English.

"Born and bred, madam." He gave her a lovely smile.

"And what brings you to Paris?"

"Football, madam. The European Cup." Aled quickly decided not to pursue this tactic as he'd momentarily forgotten who Juventus was playing. "And you?"

"Just a bit of shopping. Got to leave on Saturday unfortunately. Wish I could stay longer." Aled's phone pinged in his pocket.

"Excuse me." He took a few paces back from the bedroom furniture display.

"How's it going boyo?"

"Just talking to her now. She's leaving Paris on Saturday."

The revelation was followed by a long silence at the other end. Then "Brilliant work! I'll text Millbank Man immediately. See you downstairs in about 15 minutes."

"Where exactly?"

"Ask any of the attendants to direct you to *The Origins of the World.*"

"*Origins of the Word*? Right y'are boss." Giving Mrs al-Assad a courteous wave Aled headed for the lifts. A young female attendant on the ground floor directed him down the huge museum's central aisle, giving him a mischievous smile. He eventually encountered a large group viewing a small oil painting no more than 18" x 24". There appeared to be a suspiciously large number of teenage boys amongst the onlookers. Gustave Courbet's infamous Impressionist classic *L'Origine du Monde*, an unadorned study of a naked female torso, left nothing to the imagination. Garry nudged Aled and beckoned towards the main exit.

Garry slapped Aled heartily on the back. "Well done boyo; however did you do it? I tell you, Millbank Man's over the moon!" Aled shrugged with mock-embarrassment.

"What say we go and have some French onion soup – there's a nice little bistro I know just around the corner. We can watch the Merc from there."

"Lead on."

The friends took a quiet corner table by the window and armed with two large glasses of Beaujolais awaited their soups. "I'm just going to step outside and bring Millbank Man up to speed," Garry whispered, pocketing his mobile phone.

On his return he quietly summarised their instructions. "London's been planning this 'snatch' ever since the al-Assads quit Damascus. We're to be mere bystanders in the hotel lobby. Millbank Man says on no account are we to get involved."

"Otherwise?"

"Well, his rather undiplomatic words were: 'Unless you two want to finish up in a bloody French slammer – and you can sort your own bail out!'"

"ICC Day – let's call it – will be 10.00 hrs on Saturday morning. London's already pinpointed the hotel she's staying at – it's just around the corner from the Russian Embassy."

"And what does ICC stand for?"

"International Criminal Court. It's in The Hague. Set up by the UN about fifty years ago to track down despots and tyrants with blood on their hands. They've raised a warrant for Asma al-Assad's arrest. I'd guess it's only a tactical move – an attempt to flush out old Bashar. But they have to serve it on her in person and my man at Millbank Towers is saying that you and I need to be present to identify her to the Dutch authorities. Seems she's in good company too."

"Such as?"

"Her 'landlord' Vladimir Putin, for one. Then there's Gaddafi's son Saif al-Islam, who's been on the run for more than 12 years. Benjamin Netanyahu and Myanmar's military leader General Min Aung Hlaing are the latest additions to their Rogues' Gallery. Slobodan Milošević was one of their top scalps; died in his cell before the trial ended. I was part of the armed detail that picked up his mate Ratko Mladić. Remember him – The Butcher of Bosnia?"

"I certainly do."

Garry checked his phone, but there was nothing from London. "Old Bashar must be getting bored rigid, stuck up there in his Kremlin penthouse. I'll tell you one who did slip through the ICC's net."

"Who was that?"

"Henry Kissinger."

"No? That old bruiser!"

"Seems he was running an errand for Nixon. Back in those days many of America's international telephone links had been compromised by Soviet satellites. So Henry was the messenger, staying *incognito* at the Paris embassy."

"What happened, Garry?"

"The Dutch had got wind of the trip and successfully applied for an ICC warrant in The Hague."

"Strewth!"

"But the old fox outsmarted them. Packed his bags and hopped on a scheduled flight out of Orly the same evening."

"So what's our role on Saturday?" Aled asked.

"My man at Millbank Towers says you'll have to do the identification as you're the one who spoke to her. Just give her a nice smile, step back and nod at one of the Dutch ICC officials. Simples."

"And then what?"

Garry pulled their two prized European Cup tickets from his pocket with a grin. "Well provided it all goes smoothly and there's no fisticuffs with the local gendarmes

– we can go off to the Stade de France to watch the footie, old son!"

On the Saturday the two British agents were in place outside the four-star *L'Etoile d'Or* well before the arrival of a discreet Dutch convoy, which comprised two black SUVs with smoked windows, the lead car flying a Dutch pennant. Between them was an unmarked black Brink's-Mat-type bullion van. It was beginning to drizzle with rain.

A dark-suited diplomat led the way into the hotel's plush reception area, followed by two unsmiling officials – one male, one female. The man carried a briefcase; his colleague clutched a large manilla envelope. Garry and Aled brought up the rear and watched as the diplomat asked for Mrs al-Assad at the reception desk. In the few minutes that elapsed Garry effected discreet introductions, assuring the Dutchman that Aled would identify Asma as soon as she stepped out of the lift. The Dutchman gave a half-smile and nodded. *"Goed."*

After what seemed like an age, there was Asma al-Assad framed in the lift opening, with the Russian Embassy driver behind her laden down with packages and cases. Carrying a small posy of crimson and yellow freesia, she was dressed in white, with a caramel-coloured mohair coat slung over her shoulders. Garry gave Aled a nudge in the ribs and the Welshman nervously stepped out of the shadows and nodded a friendly salutation at the puzzled woman, making the identification.

Then, accompanied by a Dutch introduction, the warrant was duly served into her hand. The chauffeur froze, half in and half out of the lift car, as Mrs al-Assad handed him her posy, while the hotel manager remained open-mouthed and speechless. It was as if this sequence of silent moves had been endlessly plotted for an action-thriller movie. Behind him, Aled heard the click of the shutter on Garry's camera phone as it froze in time this strange, carefully-choreographed moment.

"Please to step outside," suggested the Dutch diplomat to the Syrian dictator's terrified wife. She meekly obeyed. Bowed and looking frail, she was led by the female diplomat down the steps of the hotel and up the metal steps into the back of the armoured van.

Garry nudged his partner. "Come on – let's ride up a few floors in the other lift, then find a fire escape back down before *le flic* arrives, shall we, boyo?" He had barely uttered the suggestion than a grey Citroën van, its warning klaxon blaring, came racing down the street, skidding to a halt on the wet cobbles.

Five minutes later the pair were slumped in the back of a taxi, headed for the Stade de France. Garry took his phone from his jacket pocket and quickly brought up the three hastily-grabbed screenshots he'd taken in the hotel lobby. Neither man could be identified from the images. "You managed to get my bald patch," observed Aled tartly. "So, what are you planning to do with them; give 'em to Millbank Man?"

"For the Ministry files – and his OBE? No way, José. They're far too valuable!"

"What then?"

"I've an old mate who used to be one of Murdoch's senior Picture Editors down on Canary Wharf. He's retired now but he keeps his hand in doing a bit of international syndication. Mostly *paparazzi* snaps of celebs. I reckon these'll be like gold dust if we hang onto 'em until her case comes up at The Hague." The older man gave a rueful smile and gazed out of the taxi's window as flag-waving fans, oblivious of the rain, converged on the stadium. "I think I can confidently predict, old son, that we won't need to work again!"

5

The Recital

THE cream-coloured Mercedes 190 SL convertible pulled up in front of the gates to Windsor Castle's visitors car park. David Furnish was at the wheel, with Sir Elton John seated beside him. Sir Elton held out a clutch of official passes and invitations, which an armed policeman carefully inspected, before waving the sports car in. "Park to the left of the striped bollard marked 'VISITORS' would you please, sir?" he requested, handing the paperwork back. The dashboard clock showed 3.20 pm.

Framed by an opened side entrance door was a smartly-attired official, in a crimson and gold uniform, holding a clipboard under one arm. He shook both visitors warmly by the hand. "Welcome to Windsor Castle, gentlemen." Then turning to the driver, added: "Whilst Sir Elton has his audience with Her Majesty, sir, you are very welcome to walk around the gardens." The form of words (delivered most courteously) made it clear that it was Elton alone who was to take tea with The Queen. Furnish nodded, reached into the car for his Barbour shoulder bag, and then with a nonchalant wave, headed off in the direction of the huge flower gardens which encircle the Castle's south wing. The liveried footman gestured his other visitor towards the entrance in which he had been standing.

In front of them, a long narrow top-lit panelled corridor seemed to stretch to infinity, with a crimson and gold central carpet to guide the way. The left-hand walls were panelled in oak, whilst facing them was a veritable picture gallery of The Great and The Good, stretching back several centuries.

"This is known as The Privy Counsellors Corridor, sir" the footman called back, advancing towards a pair of double doors in the distance. "This is where the Sovereign consults her Privy Counsellors."

"And where do they sit?"

"They don't, sir. They stand."

The two men had now reached the far end of the corridor, as a pair of double doors magically swung open. A liveried black footman stood beside them and bowed his head as Elton was ushered into the Royal Castle's Tea Room, with his guide following behind. A small carriage clock on the mantlepiece struck the half-hour as the footman disappeared through a door marked 'KITCHENS'.

Almost simultaneously, and from a pair of doors at the far end of the Tea Room, The Queen appeared. She was tastefully dressed in a pale blue printed blouse and matching skirt over royal-blue suede half-heels. She held a slender walking cane in her right hand and cautiously advanced towards the two men.

"Your Majesty: may I present Sir Elton John." The singer bowed his head.

"I'm so pleased to meet you after all this time, Sir Elton," The Queen intoned in her fragile voice. "Sadly, it was Charles who presided at your Investiture as I was away on a Commonwealth tour."

The Queen gave a nod to the footman who reached forward and rang a small handbell on a side table. This was clearly the signal to the kitchens that tea could now be served. The black footman reappeared, steering a gilt tea trolley, followed by a Filipino maid carrying a huge silver teapot. The Queen moved to take a place alone on a velvet-covered chaise longue, while the footman gestured to Elton to take a seat at the tea table.

Spread before them were geometrically perfect sandwiches, dainty doily-wrapped angel cakes and pre-cut slices of iced chocolate cake. In the centre of this confectionery composition was a glass stand supporting a veritable pyramid of identically sized buttered muffins, each halved. As the Filipino maid prepared a small selection for her Mistress and the footman poured the tea, The Queen advised her guest: "Do please help yourself."

The Sovereign's appetite was bird-like, washed down by a half-cup of milk-ess tea, while Elton was already on his second muffin. When host and guest had clearly eaten all they could, the two staff quietly removed all the tea things and withdrew to the kitchens.

"What I thought we might do," The Queen began hesitantly, "is to first take a look at The Ballroom next door. Though I must warn you, it's in a bit of a state at the moment!"

"Why so?" Elton enquired. "Is there to be a Ball tonight?"

"If only! No, we have the decorators in, I'm afraid. All the walls are being re-papered. In consequence, all the portraits have had to be taken down and are now standing propped against the walls. But the decorators have been told that on no account are they to move the Steinway. It's sheeted over but Gordon can soon have them removed. It has a most beautiful sound, though in an empty Ballroom, you may decide that it sounds too hollow."

"I'm more than happy to give it a go, Your Majesty," Elton enthused.

"Oh good. Well, that's settled. Let me just tell Gordon." Monarch and servant briefly conferred and the footman discreetly exited via the double doors at the far end of the Tea Room. The Monarch remained seated.

"May I just say, Sir Elton, how much my husband and I appreciated your extreme generosity last summer when you came to the rescue of poor Harry and his new fiancée? It was so kind of you to offer them hospitality at your villa in Monaco."

Elton John shook his head in mock modesty. "It was nothing, Your Majesty; David and I thought it was the least we could do."

Now the double doors had been swung back by two footmen. Gordon could be seen flicking specks of dust off the grand piano with a yellow duster. The singer stood, curious to glimpse this space for the first time. The young maid helped The Queen to her feet and accompanied her as she led the way into Windsor Castle's Ballroom.

The oak blockwork herringbone floor was criss-crossed with decorators' sheeting (all marked 'Osborne & Little') and around the walls of the cavernous space were 30 or 40 oil-painted portraits of nobility, military and statesmen who all looked on in disbelief, as if they had been deposed from their rightful positions.

Gordon was carefully folding the sheets he had removed from the Steinway as The Queen gestured for Elton to go to the keyboard. He lifted its lid and realised that in the absence of a piano stool he would have to play standing up – something he had done countless times during concerts. He looked to The Queen for confirmation and she gave him a reassuring nod.

His two hands fell lightly on the ivory keys and the instrument responded faultlessly, though the hollow 'reverberation time', caused by the absence of furnishings, couldn't be ignored. Another two chords and it all sounded eerily sombre. The pianist looked at his Patron for guidance.

"Awfully 'echoey' wouldn't you say?"

"I'm afraid so, Ma'am."

"Gordon? Go and see what state the Bechstein in the Garden Room is in, will you? I know there was a piano tuner in there only last week."

"Certainly, Your Majesty."

To fill the gap, Queen Elizabeth recounted to her visitor a brief trip she had made earlier in the week to Paddington Station to inaugurate the latest section of the long-running Crossrail underground project. "I unveiled a plaque in the foyer and was about to leave, when a railway official asked me: 'Would you like to travel on one of the new trains?'" She gave a giggle; "I could hardly refuse, could I? With difficulty we negotiated the escalator and there before us, parked at the platform, were two brand new railway carriages painted in a beautiful bright purple with ELIZABETH LINE written on their sides. In gold!"

"So where did they take you to?" Elton asked his Royal host.

"Somewhere called Gospel Oak. Then we came back."

Elton closed the Steinway's lid, returning it once again to its slumbers, as Gordon reappeared, smiling. "Everything is fine, Ma'am; and the maids have made the room ready."

He led the way diagonally across the Ballroom to yet another set of double doors, swung open to reveal a sun-drenched vista of the Castle's flower gardens, in which a group of Royal children could be seen playing under the supervision of a nanny. Discreetly stationed about ten paces away from the group was a uniformed officer of the Royal family's Personal Protection Unit. The oldest child was enthusiastically pulling up armfuls of small white lilies and handing them to the Nanny. "That's William's eldest," The Queen identified with amusement.

The smaller space they were now standing in was clearly a purpose-made recital room, as concentric arcs of upholstered chairs 'radiated' behind the ebony-black Bechstein grand, its lid lifted and propped. And this time, Elton was relieved to note, there was a piano stool! "May I?" he asked The Queen as he grasped one of the stool's handles.

"By all means."

Nervously, the world's most famous rock-pianist perched on the edge of the stool and looked down at the keyboard. He tentatively tried a couple of softly played chords. Compared to the echoey great Ballroom next door, this was a much more confined and intimate space that certainly didn't warrant stadium-type histrionics. But what to play to an audience of one (Gordon and the maid had discreetly withdrawn, closing the double doors behind them)? Two more exploratory chords. Then inspiration.

Sir Elton rocked slowly forward on the edge of the piano stool. Head lowered, his blonde mop almost brushing the empty sheet music frame. Then slowly, hesitantly, he accompanied himself into the familiar opening bars of *Your Song*.

Two more verses flowed effortlessly. Then Sir Elton rested his hands on the keys while the final notes floated away. After a pause The Queen graciously nodded her approval. "Thank you so much."

"The pleasure was all mine, Ma'am."

Gordon gave a discreet cough and glanced at the carriage clock. "Don't forget your Red Boxes, Ma'am."

"Boxes?"

"We didn't finish Friday's, if you remember. Whitehall are sending a courier at 6."

"How very tiresome," observed the Monarch.

Elton's leave-taking of the Monarch was slow and dignified. In a strange way he had found playing a short impromptu recital to one had been as nerve-wracking as to a full-to-capacity O2 Arena. He gave a dignified bow and (using Gordon as a model) attempted to leave the Tea Room walking backwards!

David Furnish was already seated behind the wheel of the Mercedes. They clasped hands but didn't speak – his partner sensing that all had gone well. He reversed from the parking space and just before selecting first gear the driver gesticulated with his thumb to the car's rear radio aerial. Firmly secured by raffia was a bunch of white Royal lilies.

6

Heroes and Martyrs

CIVIC sculpture, freely visible in public spaces, had long been one of his passions. Cities like Rome and Paris abound with them in squares and gardens ('public realm' was a New Age term he heartily disapproved of), usually in stone or bronze and often larger-than-life. The Romans seem to favour dousing their civic tributes in water from fountains, while the Parisians frequently mounted their heroes and heroines in the centre of busy road traffic junctions. For some unknown reason, Sir Edwin Lutyens chose to site his sombre London Cenotaph between two busy Whitehall carriageways.

Historian Mark Armitage had been invited by an English tourist board to pen a compact walking tour for one of its publications featuring the capital's best civic sculptures. Before setting off on his statuary survey, he had consulted the Reference Library of the Royal Institute of British Architects to see just how many he'd need to witness. English Heritage alone, he discovered, looked after the capital's Top 40, most of which were located in Westminster, many in Parliament Square and often glaringly out of scale with each other (Churchill and Mandela being prime examples). The most inaccessible one was going to be General de Gaulle, stuck on a solitary plinth in Carlton Gardens, facing the 'grace and favour' residence that the British government had to provide for him during his three-year wartime exile.

Mark's long 'shortlist' ran to more than 50 statues, though in some quarters such as Parliament Square, he would find the likes of Churchill and Gandhi rubbing shoulders with Abraham Lincoln and Nelson Mandela. For many years a surprise hit with tourists – probably because of its 'accessibility' – was Lawrence Holofcener's *Allies*, a strikingly realistic bronze capturing Franklin D Roosevelt and Winston Churchill in animated conversation, seated on a wooden bench at the bottom of London's Bond Street.

Military and political figures were invariably favoured above popular celebrities, doubtless because it was the Great and The Good who made such choices. There are said to be about 30 Beatles statues dotted around the globe, though none in the capital. The writer decided that London's excellent bus routes (the classy Routemaster had recently been introduced) would be the perfect mode of transport. Mark clocked up just under 40 on his first day.

After viewing Decimus Burton's ceremonial arch in the centre of the busy Hyde Park Corner junction, facing the Duke of Wellington's London residence Apsley House (which includes the largest bronze statue in Europe), he opted to walk north through Hyde Park to Marble Arch and there try to find a quiet café for a coffee and a sandwich.

He crossed into Cumberland Place, dismissing the rather glitzy Cumberland Hotel as being beyond his budget and ventured northwards, past the elegant late-Regency terraces of what was planned as (but never executed) Regents Circus. Glancing diagonally across the quiet side street he saw shafts of angled sunlight falling on an extraordinary monument. One that he hadn't included on his list.

A huge vertical slab of patinated bronze, at least four metres high, towered above a life-sized male figure, with an overcoat draped over his shoulders. There was no plinth or carved citation. He crossed the street to take a closer look. The sculptor's name – Philip Jackson – was etched into the ground the figure was placed on, with several small posies of fresh flowers laid at his feet. Around about the statue's shoulder height the name RAOUL WALLENBERG was engraved on the slab – a name he didn't recognise from his researches.

Moving around to the back of the bronze slab, Mark discovered that the sculptor seemed to have placed his subject against a veritable 'wall' of documents. The effect was that - from the front - Mr Wallenberg was merely taking the morning air, so to speak, protected by his overcoat. However, concealed behind him were several thousand travel documents, all wrapped in sealed bundles.

Since there was no signed information to explain this conundrum, he crossed to one of the offices in the small close which was directly behind the statue. A helpful receptionist handed Mark a single-page information sheet headed WALLENBERG MONUMENT, in which much fascinating detail – not to mention several unanswered questions – was set out.

It explained that the Swedish architect Raoul Wallenberg had been appointed a senior diplomat during the closing stages of the Second World War. He was alerted to the plight of the many thousands of Jewish people, who were being transported by train across Europe to the Nazis' detested concentration camps, on the instructions of Adolf Eichmann. With commendable bravery and speed, Wallenberg organised the design, printing and distribution of thousands of realistic-looking fake travel permits (*Schutz-Passes*), which some historians estimate may have saved the lives of as many as 10,000 European jews in Budapest.

This Swedish hero-diplomat's own demise is less well-documented - one might almost say obliterated. Despite his diplomatic immunity, Wallenberg was taken into custody by the Soviet authorities in 1944, then transferred to the NKVD's notorious Lubyanka detention centre in Moscow, where his death was officially recorded as a 'cardiac arrest'. What seems so utterly awful about Raoul Wallenburg's end is that it remains unexplained. He entered the Lubyanka and just vanished. Numerous official pan-European enquiries failed to establish just how - and when - the Swedish hero met his end.

Mark walked back to the Cumberland Hotel and purchased a small posy of spring flowers in the lobby, which he returned and left on the ground beside Raoul Wallenberg's feet. His chance encounter with the martyr had left him rather nonplussed. Do we 'over-eulogise' our national political heroes, to the detriment of many martyrs, he wondered? Joan of Arc, Tom Simpson, Bruce McLaren and Alan Turing (whose pioneering work on the Enigma codebreaking machine almost certainly foreshortened the length of WWII, before he took his own life). Even poor Violette Szabo – Britain's most highly-decorated WWII woman combatant - had a witness to her execution as she knelt in a bleak corridor in Ravensbrück.

On his return from his high-speed monument tour, Mark found a message waiting for him on his answerphone. It was from a horticulturist friend. "You must be sure to include the new Diana memorial garden behind Kensington Palace in your survey, Mark. It's simply stunning." He dropped everything and dashed across to W8.

And he certainly wasn't disappointed. Beside a rectangular pool in what is known as the Sunken Garden, sculptor Ian Rank-Broadley had set a group of four bronze figures: Princess Diana, surrounded by three children. But it was the meticulously landscaped and planted flower beds, 'framing' the pool, which created such a perfect composition. Ingeniously, the sculptor and the Palace gardeners had contrived to encircle their composition with a quick-growing yew hedge, in which 'viewing niches' permitted the public to admire the composition, without venturing down into the garden itself. It all had a very theatrical feel: Diana, down there 'on stage' surrounded by three anonymous children, being 'observed' from the openings in the hedging, all like small theatrical boxes.

The article which eventually appeared was clearly strongly influenced by that chance encounter with the Swedish hero Wallenberg in Great Cumberland Place. And Mark concluded that his emotional response may have been the reason why he never received another commission from that publication. 'Come and admire our heroes; they are all around you' it concluded. 'Our martyrs are a little harder to find.'

7

The Snowman

"WHAT about this one?" He flung an opened holiday cottages brochure across to his niece who was seated on the sofa opposite.

They were in the early stages of tracking down a suitable furnished country cottage to rent (with his sister) for a week during the girl's Easter school holidays. Scarlett spun the booklet around to examine a colour photo of the thatched cottage's exterior. It certainly seemed to fit the bill.

'*Set in private grounds overlooking a small lake, this well-insulated two-bedroomed property – a former Victorian summer house - sleeps four. Its furnishings are comfortable and traditional, with a beautifully-equipped kitchen and luxury shower room,*' she read out. "And guess what, Uncle?"

"What's that?"

'*Pets, such as small dogs, permitted!*' she called out gleefully. "So Ben can come too!" It seemed the matter had been settled.

The tiny hamlet of Badger's Wood was tucked away in a fold in the Shropshire Hills, a mere 40 miles from where they lived in the Midlands – though without his SUV's trusty satellite navigation Ted Stevens doubted whether they would ever have found it. Ominously, in a corner of the dashboard screen, was a snowflake symbol and the four-word warning: 'SNOWFALLS LIKELY IN SHROPSHIRE'.

He stopped the car to let his niece get out to open the five-bar gate and collect an empty jam jar in which the front door keys to the cottage had been left by the landlords. There was already a light dusting of snow on the gravelled drive. Ben shifted nervously in the rear luggage area, sensing that the hour-long journey was nearly over. They rolled slowly forwards to stop in front of Badger Cottage.

The letting agents had certainly done this compact little Victorian cottage justice. Everything was neat and cosy and some form of underfloor heating had ensured it was warm and welcoming. Ted unloaded the car, Scarlett decided on the allocation of the bedrooms, and her mother had soon mastered the controls of the kitchen's air fryer to heat up the prepared lasagne she'd brought. Beside the landlords' Welcome card there was even a bottle of rosé wine for them to toast their successful arrival.

The trio took their cooked lunch in relative calm, while Ben paced up and down in expectation. Ted was relieved to see that there was no snow falling and the sun had now come out. Clearing away the dishes Sarah looked to her brother, as Party Leader, to suggest what their plans should be.

"Well, first off, we've all got to wrap up well as it's bound to be cold out there. And in case that lake is now covered by ice under the snow – and I for one don't fancy having to fish Ben from its icy depths – let's stay on the other side of the cottage. Where we first drove in?" This sensible but boring suggestion was met by a glum face from the eight-year-old. "Good idea" enthused her mother, coming to his rescue. "And warm clothes, scarves, bobble hats and woolly mittens, please!"

"Seconded!" he swiftly added. "And if we go halfway down the drive to where that chestnut tree is where we came in, we could build a big snowman if you like?" he told Scarlett. The snowman offer did the trick.

In a lean-to outhouse he sorted out some 'decorative extras' which he knew would animate their snowman. Some nice round pieces of coke could be his coat buttons and a crooked hazel stick was removed from a pile of kindling wood to use as his pipe. Scarlett stood in the shed's doorway, brandishing a long raw carrot. "Mum says this can be his nose." All that was missing was his hat and scarf.

With Ben barking furiously at every spade full of snow that was dug, the figure quickly took shape. His coke buttons were added and a pair of smooth granite stones served as the toecaps of his boots. Their snowman was now over two metres tall and it was left to Sarah to add his carrot nose. The three stepped back to admire their handiwork. "There's one thing still missing," Ted told his niece.

"What's that, Uncle?"

"I think he needs a warm collar for the top of his overcoat. To keep out the cold." The little girl pulled a face of bafflement, but her mother set off back to the kitchen, shortly returning with a decorated crimson and gold tea towel – a record of the recent Royal marriage of William and Kate. She neatly folded the towel into a long strip and wrapped it around the snowman's throat. Scarlett clapped with glee at the transformation. "What about his hat?" she asked.

"Let's go and have a cup of tea," Sarah suggested diplomatically, "and I'll see what I can find in the cottage's kitchen." As a trained milliner, Ted had confidence that his sister would come up with the answer. Sure enough, after they'd polished off some home-baked shortbread biscuits, washed down with tea, she placed a very convincing 'cheese-cutter' cap on the table, fashioned and pinned from a rolled-up check duster borrowed from the cottage's cleaning cupboard. "In these parts they're known as 'rat catcher's hats'," she told her daughter.

Back outside, they duly added Bernard the Snowman's hat, adding a spare pair of Scarlett's woolly mittens to keep his hands warm. The figure was so realistic that they could almost see smoke rising from his long hazelwood pipe. "Right team: let's make a quick circuit of the lake, shall we?" Ted suggested. "But I'm afraid Ben's going to have to stay on the lead." In line astern they trudged off towards Badger's Wood lake.

Their 'circuit' took a good hour, undisturbed by any other visitors but enlivened by a cacophony of sounds from the various birds that had clustered around the lake's edge, clearly baffled by the overnight appearance of the snow blanket. A small flock of geese were angrily protesting at being denied access to the water, backed up by some noisy seagulls (always in the front line of avian protests).

The last section back to the cottage was a long ascent up a flight of granite steps. Sarah and her brother slumped down on an iron bench at the summit, while Scarlett insisted on going around to the front of the cottage to check that Bernard was all right. Ben followed her.

It was a good ten minutes before the girl returned. She snuggled up to her mother, who asked: "Everything OK with Bernard, darling?"

"Sort of."

"Sort of? What's wrong – is he starting to melt?" The little girl shook her head.

"Then what is it?"

"He's moved! He's nearer to the cottage's front porch now."

"Moved?" Ted queried.

"Yup. Come and see." Followed by Ben the three skirted Badger Cottage to reach the front drive. But their beautifully-crafted snow sculpture was no longer standing beneath the chestnut tree at the end of the drive where they'd built it. Unmarked or damaged, it now stood a couple of metres in front of the cottage's small lean-to porch. Aided or unassisted, Bernard had moved 20 metres closer to their accommodation. The doughty snowman's headgear now looked more like a white woolly tam o'shanter than a rat catcher's cap. Sarah and Scarlett both looked to Ted for an explanation. Cocking his head on one side, even Ben seemed bewildered.

"A prank by local kids?" he offered half-heartedly. But they smiled with mock-derision. "You'll have to do better than that!" Scarlett chuckled. "Next thing, you'll be saying it was the Snow Fairies!"

It was left to Sarah to 'break' the impasse. "How about bubble-and-squeak with chips for supper? I think I've got the hang of the kitchen's air fryer." The suggestion was supported unanimously. Pudding would be tinned peaches and ice cream.

Having divested themselves of all their 'outdoor gear', the consensus was not to venture outside again, especially as more large falling snowflakes could be seen through the living room window, presaging another overnight snowfall. After desultory TV 'channel-hopping' failed to turn up anything entertaining to watch, they decided to follow Sarah's suggestion and have an early night. Scarlett offered to walk Ben down to the front gate for his last exercise of the day. Ten minutes later she and a snow-flecked Sheltie returned.

"Everything OK outside, Pickle?" her mother enquired. "I see it's snowing hard again."

"That's not all."

"How'd you mean, darling?"

"Now Bernard's taken shelter in our porch!"

Ted and Sarah's feeble explanations for how an inert snowman could move 50 yards down the driveway were greeted by the girl with derision, though thankfully she found the incident amusing rather than sinister.

Scarlett was awake at 6.00 am the next morning and pulled back the bedroom curtains to reveal that another heavy overnight snowfall had 're-fashioned' the grounds surrounding the little cottage. She slipped into the kitchenette to make Sarah and her uncle two mugs of tea.

"There's some strange puddles on the floor," the girl told her mother.

"Bother! That'll be Ben, I suppose."

"I don't think so. Come and see."

Sarah and her daughter stared down at four identically sized circular pools of water, which made a line from the entrance hall door to the kitchen table. On the table was last night's coffee mugs and an empty plate containing biscuit crumbs. Ted joined them, then strolled out into the hall and swung the front door half open. With a mischievous smile he beckoned Scarlett to come and see the snowman.

Bernard still stood guard under the porch roof. But his snowy-white chin beneath his hazel stick 'pipe' was now liberally dusted with biscuit crumbs.

8

Escape from Mariupol

MARIUPOL, the industrial port city in the Donbas region, had a pre-conflict population of 400,000. Perched on the north bank of the Sea of Azov, the sprawling 11-square kilometre Azovstal Iron and Steel Works had once been the city's principal employer, at its peak annually producing more than six million tons of high-grade steel, exported across Europe. It was said to have originally been built to withstand nuclear attack.

In May 2022, after the Russian-Ukrainian conflict was barely three months old, the labyrinthian tunnels and cellars beneath the giant steelworks were to became shelter to more than a thousand Mariupol adults and children, displaced by horrific day and night bombardment from Russian artillery and drones.

The citizens of Mariupol shared their refuge with 1000 Ukrainian troops. Its reinforced underground concrete walls constantly trembled. Above ground, Russian ground and aerial bombardment systematically laid waste the steelworkers' apartment blocks. Some 20,000 Russian soldiers – many raw recruits – were hurriedly moved to this key frontline position to compensate for the debacle of President Putin's farcical 3,000-tank invasion.

During daylight hours, few brave Mariupol souls ventured out into the open – and then only to retrieve belongings such as children's bedding or medical supplies from the rubble that was formerly their homes. Or to risk drawing fresh water from wells without being picked off by

Russian snipers. One especially heinous Russian ruse was to park a supermarket trolley, laden with packaged food, close to the factory gates. Anyone foolish enough to try to retrieve goods from the trolley would be picked off by the sharpshooters. For two months the citizens of Mariupol survived life underground without daylight, with basic foods and water strictly rationed. The living became cooks, medics, childminders and undertakers, until a UN-brokered bus convoy finally took the shell-shocked survivors to safety.

But before that historic day one man, a widowed pensioner named Oleg, had resolved to break out, despite the dire warnings of the Ukrainian troops who were sharing the underground shelter with the townspeople. The old man had made up a compact knapsack of essential items and told them he intended to make a marathon trek with his dog Lulu to a friend's safe haven inland in the unoccupied northern Donetsk Oblast region. Nervous of being holed up so dangerously close to the Russian border, Oleg's plan was to quit Mariupol and head north. Troops in the steelworks' basement were reporting that the territory had so far escaped heavy Russian bombing. Formerly Stalino, the city was given the new name by Nikita Krushchev in 1961. Oleg fondly remembered an Easter service he had once attended in its Baroque Configuration Cathedral.

"We'll take it one day at a time," Oleg assured the doubters who were gathered around the factory's entrance to see him off. "I know the road well, having driven there many times when I was younger. There's only one river to cross – the Kalmius - and there won't be any Russian tanks to avoid, as most of them have broken down!" he joked as he bade farewell to his friends, who would stay marooned in their Faustian labyrinth. Most were convinced they'd never see the old man again.

Mid-morning. Man and dog ascended a gentle incline between neatly cultivated wheat fields. But the vista directly ahead, whilst it clearly showed an azure river crossing their field of vision up ahead, included no bridge linking the two banks. Just piles of concrete rubble and twisted steel. Oleg took shelter in case the ruined crossing was being guarded by Russian snipers and scanned the banks with his ancient field glasses. But carrion crows and long-billed waders were the only 'guards' he could discern. He fished out his final chocolate bar, broke it in half and shared it with his faithful little dog.

"So what's it to be my little lovely? Obviously, there's no turning back now. That's a fast-flowing river down there and I haven't the foggiest idea where the next crossing is, upstream or down." Lulu cocked her head on one side as if weighing up the consequences. Suddenly and silently, without warning, a slim all-black rocket-shaped object sped over them towards the horizon, far quicker than any bird could fly – even a hawk in hot pursuit. In the fleeting moment that he could focus on it, Oleg guessed this alien projectile was less than a metre long with tiny projecting wingtips. Lulu looked up to her master for an explanation, but he simply shook his head in disbelief.

The old man slowly packed up the bag and hitched it over one shoulder as they made a move to edge closer to the water's edge. He certainly wasn't going to let go of the little dog's lead; the water was fast-flowing and deep, swollen by spring rainfall.

Having always previously driven over it on the road bridge - and not being especially 'marine minded' - at close quarters Oleg found this 20-metre-wide barrier even more intimidating than it had looked back up on the hillock. There were certainly no moored or sunken boats – or any other sort of craft – nor any wooden bridge debris. Nor any helpful human with whom to share the problem. Once again he fished out his binoculars.

Up ahead on the other bank, some two or three kilometres along a winding road, he could just make out a thin trail of smoke coming from a small wooden cottage, its weatherboard walls painted with black pitch. There was even an empty rocking chair on the porch and it seemed highly likely that the owners had not evacuated. It all looked very inviting.

It was now 3.00 pm. He gave himself two hours to come up with a solution to safely cross the river – probably with Lulu stowed inside his waterproof jacket – and then to throw themselves on the mercy of these distant homesteaders.

The river's shingle beach and shallow foreshore offered nothing in the way of usable debris that might help Oleg and Lulu get across. Concrete never floats. But then suddenly - a breakthrough!

Sticking out from beneath a huge broken slab of the bridge structure was a welcoming corner of bright orange pine. A wooden door. Probably all that remained of a timber-built tool store that had once stood beneath one of the bridge's arches. Oleg ran along the shingle and yanked it out excitedly.

"When is a door not a door?" he asked the little dog. Lulu cocked her head on one side.

"Why, when it's a raft, my lovely!" the old man cried excitedly as he pulled the solid pine door free of its debris. "And with plenty of room for two!"

Heavy-duty cables from the bridge's overhead lighting still hung across the water to the farthest bank. These, Oleg quickly decided, he would use to guide them across on their 'raft' – so long as they didn't snap under the strain.

With his knapsack repacked and Lulu tucked safely inside his zipped-up anorak, the old man nervously slid their raft down to the water's edge. The next manoeuvre was like something out of *Baywatch*. With the lighting cable wrapped twice around his body, Oleg kicked the door into the rushing waters and stepped onto its solid pine boards, legs akimbo. He stood erect, like a seasoned surfer. Immediately they were afloat.

He tugged the lighting cable with all his might, checking any rush downstream. Mercifully, the plastic cables held. And in less than ten minutes the 'ferryman' had skilfully navigated them across the waters without incident.

Inside his coat, he sensed the mongrel remaining still. Until the moment when their door-raft beached itself on the cobblestones of the far bank. Then it barked with delight. It was just before 5.00 pm. Gazing longingly at the enticing plume of smoke coiling skywards from the far-off cottage, they set forth with gusto.

Oleg's new hosts, an elderly farming couple, couldn't have been more welcoming, insisting that he stayed the night. "And in the morning, after breakfast, I'll drive you to your friend's house in my old Lada. There's no point in walking any further!"

Oleg's reunion with his university companion Tomas was as welcoming as it had been with the farming couple. Tomas – now the proud owner of an Apple mobile phone – insisted that the world needed to be informed of the plight of the surviving people of Mariupol. Within an hour he had hooked up with a journalist friend in Belgrade and an hour later that contact had opened up a news channel with a Paris-based European correspondent of *France Soir*.

By nightfall, the plight of the stoic people of Mariupol would be known throughout Europe, achieved through the dogged determination of one man. A fortnight later, the first of several UN-brokered bus convoys began the relief of the Siege of Mariupol.

9

WC2 Bloodsports

ENGLISH public schoolboys, especially when hunting in packs, will comfortably give the huntsmen's hounds a run for their money. Peter was introduced to the legendary Schmidt's Restaurant, in London's Charlotte Street gastronomic quarter, when he was still an impoverished Fifth Form schoolboy.

The gloomy first-floor German-owned emporium was famous for two things: the food was cheap (way under the benchmark of the Lyons Corner House chain) and the waiters were always rude. Whereas the petite, smiling Lyons waitresses would invariably ask: "Good afternoon, gentlemen! And what may I get for you to eat?", in Schmidt's, by contrast, after an interminable delay, a surly, unkempt waiter might approach your table and enquire gruffly: "You want something to eat?", as if questioning whether you had entered the establishment mistakenly thinking it was a men's outfitters. Their black Schmidt's aprons were always well stained and the creased and the greased menu card would remain firmly by the waiter's side, pre-empting some complicated quiz ("What is the soup of the day?" or "What exactly is *Kalbshaxe*, waiter?"). The uncarpeted floor creaked and seating at the tables was on high-backed, unupholstered Tyrolean wooden benches.

Peter loved all this cut-and-thrust and quickly learned from his school chums the finer 'duelling points' which would inevitably 'floor' their poor foreign adversaries. Using a non-Germanic language – *"hors d'oeuvre* for me please – with some *pommes frites*" – invariably drew blood. Herr Schmidt himself (an uncanny precursor of the legendary foul-mouthed Gordon Ramsey) remained shrouded behind black curtains – like a Mystic Meg - in the Payments Booth at the top of the stairs down to the street. The owner's plaintively-posted request: 'Please have the right money for payment' was an open invitation for the tendering of large-denomination banknotes, resulting in Germanic curses.

The ground floor of Schmidt's German food emporium was taken up by a huge brightly lit delicatessen, brimming over with chocolate and marzipan goodies at Christmastime, presided over by Herr Schmidt's cheerful sister Maria. Close by, arty Fitzrovia offered countless cafés and restaurants, several small independent bookshops and art galleries, and at the junction with Rathbone Place was the best-stocked newsagent in central London. Here Peter knew he could always get the latest issue of Spain's principal bullfighting weekly *Las Corridas de Toros*. Not a stone's throw away to the south, was Soho's legendary 'Gay Hussar' Hungarian restaurant, a watering hole popular with Leftist politicians like Aneurin Bevan, Barbara Castle and Michael Foot.

Despite its dubious reputation for service, Schmidt's attracted an impressive clientele. T S Eliot was a regular customer and there was even a rumour that the German Ambassador von Ribbentrop had once been spotted in a quiet corner of the restaurant. Staff were mostly former PoWs. Though the Second World War had officially been over for more than a year, it is possible that Schmidt's proximity to the University of London's Senate House (commandeered during wartime by Lord Beaverbrook as the government's Ministry of Information) was more than a coincidence. George Orwell and his wife had both worked there (it is said that a wag once labelled a broom cupboard Room 101). The gaunt 19-storey Portland stone building on

Bloomsbury's Russell Square was designed by the London Underground's famous Modernist architect Charles Holden. It had been an open secret towards the end of the hostilities that Hitler had expressed his intention of making Senate House his *Reichstag* once he marched into London.

On a warm spring morning during the Easter half-term the five friends met up at Schmidt's, with 'waiter baiting' high on the agenda. This lunchtime they were to be joined by the legendary Jumbo Bates – captain of the school's First XI cricket team, a veritable wizard behind the wickets and a most considerate coach with juniors who were just starting to learn the game.

Bates cheerily approached the group's table in the first-floor dining room, proudly clutching a large brown paper parcel marked 'Lilywhites'. "My new pads for next season – Leslie Compton specials! I saw him batting with his brother Denis at the Oval last Saturday." he announced, thrusting the package under the table and taking a seat. "And that's not all, gentlemen…"

"So what else, Jumbo? Spill the beans, old man!" demanded Peter. Jumbo was a master tactician, both on and off the field.

Half-concealing a smirk behind the menu, Jumbo announced in a stage whisper: "Passing through the delicatessen downstairs just now, my eye was caught by a very tasty-looking collection of nurses. Six in all; from Great Ormond Street Children's Hospital by the looks of their uniforms. They seemed to be buying cakes for some sort of celebration; an engagement party, I dare say." The attentive group had already read his mind – but waited for instructions. "What say we invite 'em all up here for lunch? All those in favour?" Following the group's roar of acclamation to the suggestion, Jumbo headed for the stairs, calling back: "Tell miserable Igor over there we'll order when I get back!"

The skipper was as good as his word and less than 10 minutes later proudly returned, followed in line astern by six remarkably attractive hospital nurses, clutching their boxed purchases from the downstairs delicatessen and all blushing with embarrassment. Igor was summoned with his threadbare menu while Jumbo assumed the role of Master of Ceremonies and made the necessary introductions.

The lunch hour sped past and it was soon time for the schoolboys to bid farewell to the Heavenly Hospital Sextet (after the furtive exchange of telephone numbers), which had so fortuitously dropped into their laps in the legendary Schmidt's emporium.

10

The Monastery

HE cautiously opened his eyes, to be greeted by dazzling sunlight streaming in through the sash window beyond his bed. He slowly moved his aching head left and right. The room was empty. Its vaulted ceiling and dark-stained rafters led him to think that he must be at the top of a very old house or mansion.

The bed's neatly-turned, pink-and-white counterpane bore a woven crest with the initials 'B A'. On the left-hand side of the bed was a small mahogany table bearing the familiar accoutrements of a nursing home: a water carafe and tumbler, a clock and an alarm button on a chord. The floor was carpeted with a beige herringbone Wilton, overlaid by long Kazak runners on either side of the bed.

On the back of a chrome clipboard hanging from the rail at the foot of his bed, the confused patient read the capitalised instruction 'NIL BY MOUTH'. He went to reach for a cleansing mouth wash before deciding that the admonitory 'nil' might even apply to water.

The door into the room creaked tentatively open to reveal a small Filipino nurse. Half-in and half-out of the room, she nervously enquired: "So, you're awake?"

"Only half-awake, nurse." Then after a pause – as she entered the room and stood at his bedside – adding: "So where exactly am I?"

"Broadlands Abbey."

"Is it a hospital?"

"No sir, this is a private nursing home. It was once a Benedictine Monastery."

"Whereabouts?"

"In Herefordshire, sir."

"And did I come here of my own accord?"

"You were brought here by relatives, sir."

"How did we arrive?"

"In a black Daimler, sir."

He nodded. "That'll have been cousin Esmond's. And who else was there?"

"Apart from the chauffeur? Only an elderly lady in a wheelchair."

"Mmmm. My half-sister, Agnes. She's been trying to have me put away for years!"

As the young nurse moved around the bed, smoothing out creases in the counterpane, the man heard the distant sound of an electronic klaxon: not a fire alarm; more like the signal used on cruise ships to indicate a mealtime. By the time shown on his bedside alarm clock – 08.03 - it must be for the service of breakfast. He heard a trolley rattle past his bedroom door but no-one entered. After initialling the blank sheet on his clipboard, the nurse left.

The confused patient let his head sink back into the pillows, reflecting on the delightful items – all banned – that had probably been on the trolley that had just passed his door: porridge, hot toast and marmalade, perhaps even scrambled egg. Fresh coffee.

He ran his eye around the room, noting several old framed prints hanging on the walls. All Victorian, he guessed. A faded sepia print of what he assumed was the main entrance to Broadlands Abbey showed a Gothic stone arch, with one of its studded entrance doors swung half-open, 'guarded' by an official in a frock coat.

A second print showed a traditional rural landscape with cattle in the middle distance, grazing beyond a ha-ha. A third was a group photograph of around a dozen craftsmen, standing in line on a terrace. Many carried the tools of their trade: masons holding chisels and mallets, carpenters holding their saws. Most wore hats. In the centre of the group stood the architect in a stove pipe hat, be-whiskered and unsmiling. 'Almost certainly one of the Pugins,' the patient thought to himself. Augustus and his sons had reaped a rich harvest of fees designing country houses for Herefordshire's gentry he recalled, Eastnor Castle being a prime example.

He wracked his brain for anything he knew or remembered about Broadlands Abbey, but his long-term recall would not oblige. Here he was, stranded - alone and hungry - in what appeared to be a privately-run sanitorium for the well-to-do. Deciding he needed to know a little bit more about why he was being 'detained' at Broadlands Abbey, he grasped the alarm button and gave it a long press.

Several minutes elapsed before the bedroom door opened, revealing an unsmiling male Indian doctor, with a stethoscope around his neck. The patient squinted, but his visitor's name badge was too small to read. "How may I help?" the doctor asked.

"You may help," the disgruntled patient spluttered, "by explaining to me why exactly I am here! Is there something wrong with me? And whose idea was it that I should be admitted to Broadlands Abbey? Certainly not mine!" As the medico moved around to the end of the bed to consult the blank record sheet, the frustrated patient added: "And what's with the 'Nil by Mouth' nonsense?"

There was, of course, nothing on the patient's record sheet that would assist the doctor in answering any of the questions. Blandly, he autographed and dated the blank space directly beneath the nurse's. Then he cleared his throat. "Only the Director can answer your query about your present medical condition, sir. And the Nil by Mouth instruction is merely precautionary." He rehung the board on the bedrail, where it rocked gently on its chrome clip, adding unapologetically: "The Director is presently away in London at a national healthcare conference convened by the new Secretary of State for Health. He is unlikely to return to Broadlands before Monday at the earliest."

"So who's holding the fort in his absence? Presumably in a place of this size you can run to a Deputy Director?"

"He died last month and has not yet been replaced."

Exasperated, the patient swivelled his head on his pillow away from the doctor to glare out of the window. "How very convenient! Meanwhile, I'm to starve!" There was silence, as the two protagonists recognised that they had reached deadlock. Or, in chess terms, stalemate.

"Will there be anything further?" the medico asked in barely concealed terms of insouciance. The frustrated patient wondered whether the doctor had ever read any of Wodehouse's *Blandings* novels.

The confused, disoriented and extremely hungry patient was awoken from his light slumbers some hours later by the sounds of ferocious barking from the gardens below. 'For *Blandings* read *Baskerville Hall*', the man thought to himself. He heard a vehicle drive away.

The unhelpful Indian doctor now re-entered the room, carrying a long brown envelope. Hungrier than ever – both for answers and sustenance - his chess adversary sat bolt upright in bed, relishing a 'rematch'. "What's that you've got there?" he sneered. "My first week's fees?"

"It just arrived by Special Delivery, sir. I took the liberty of contacting the Director in London." The Indian doctor handed the unopened manilla wallet to the patient. "He says you should read it at once."

The man cautiously withdrew a dozen closely typed sheets and handed them to the patient without commenting. The bundle, bearing an embossed coat-of-arms, was headed 'MENTAL HEALTH ACT 1963 – Application for Formal Sectioning'. The patient's full name was typed underneath. Flipping through to the final page the patient found a replica of the same coat of arms. And scrawled across it in black ink in large black capital letters were the words: 'APPLICATION NOT UPHELD'. It was signed: 'Sir Giles Ballingham JP'.

"It's your unconditional discharge, actually sir."

"So I see. Well, whatever could have brought about this dramatic change in my 'treatment'?" the man asked aloud with undisguised irony. His feuding family's vile campaign of tyranny, which had been fermenting for years, was finally ended.

"While I'm packing, I'd like you to ring for a taxi," he told the doctor. "I've certainly no intention of going home in that bloody hearse!"

11

The Seagull

A GROUP of us had opted for a holiday excursion in a hired motor cruiser on the Norfolk Broads. It was the summer vacation prior to our final year's cramming for some good exam results, which would ease us all gently into commerce, trade or the professions. My father (a quantity surveyor) intended me to follow in his footsteps, though I had rather more grandiose ideas of becoming a rural property developer. As we cruised each day through the flat Fenlands, I had been surprised by the number of semi-derelict farmhouses we saw – many with dilapidated barns - dotted across the East Anglian landscape.

Brian was my closest friend on that trip, destined to become apprenticed in his father's building business. As he grudgingly put it: "I'll be 'on the tools' for a year, mate, while you're comfortably sat behind a desk learning about surveying from text books!"

Our other mutual interest (passion would be nearer the mark) was Bob Dylan, whose career we had avidly followed through his albums, writings and all-too-rare UK performances. I had ticket stubs to prove that I'd been at eight of his concerts.

Brian rang me one Friday evening. "What say we drive up to Norfolk this weekend and have a bit of a mooch around?"

"With a view to what, exactly?"

"Well, you said yourself at the time when we were cruising, that the area seemed to be littered with derelict farmhouses and broken barns. I bet we could pick one up for a song.”

“But I don’t want to live in a rat-infested hovel on The Broads! I’m scheduled to start my studies at Westminster Tech in September.”

“Weekends? I’ve run the idea past Dad and he says he might be willing to help out financially.”

“Well all I can say, Brian, is that you are extremely fortunate to have such a generous father. Mine’s as tight as a duck’s arse in winter, who regularly forgets to give me any pocket money.”

But Brian was a good talker and he eventually won me round to the idea of doing a lightening tour of the North Norfolk coast. “There’s an old Regency pile up that way called Holkham Hall I wouldn’t mind taking a look at,” he added. “It’s near King’s Lynn, where I’m sure there’ll be loads of estate agents whose brains we can pick.”

“How do we get up there?”

“Dad says I can borrow his pickup.” To save money, we elected to camp and the following weekend set off for Norfolk.

“Stiffquay, north of Cromer, sounds as if it might fit your general description, gentlemen” the helpful estate agent assured us, pulling some printed particulars from a filing cabinet and placing them in front of us. The trio of unappealing black-and-white images at the top of the page showed a lop-sided timber-clad barn with a semi-derelict cart shed alongside. Both had seen better days and it looked as if a good ‘blow’ from the North Sea would probably flatten them.

“It is said to have once been a Winnowing Barn,” the agent added helpfully. “But un-listed, which is in your favour, gentlemen. Thought to date from around 1800.”

“What’s that tall chimney in the background?” I asked.

“That’s a redundant Victorian pumping station, sir. It once helped reduce the Fens’ water levels.”

"And how much land goes with it?" Brian asked.

"Only half an acre. But of course, it has a waterfront boundary to the east."

"And moorings?" I asked. He shook his head.

Brian rolled up the particulars and tucked them in his fisherman's satchel. "How long has it been on the market?"

The agent stroked his chin, attempting to appear helpful, though recognising that this shrewd would-be purchaser had reserved the most revealing question until the end. "Errm, I'd say about two years."

Brian waited until we were outside the estate agent's office before giving me a broad wink. "Fancy some North Sea cod and chips, old son?" he asked.

"Rather!"

We consumed our snack seated on an estuary wall beside King's Lynn's famous Customs House.

"Rum do, wouldn't you say?" my friend observed.

"Why's that, mate.?"

"No offers in two years and as cheap as Kings Lynn chips. There's got to be something wrong with it!"

There was certainly plenty wrong with it. To start with, the two buildings – winnowing barn and cart shed – were in a perilously-dilapidated state. The views landward were flat and uninspiring (made bleaker by the sentinel-like chimney of the old pumping station) while the views out towards the Wash and the North Sea were just as grim. The onset of driving rain soon made us decide to cancel our plan to camp!

From then on, matters seemed to take on a momentum of their own. A week later Brian took his father up to the site for a second opinion and with his help sketched out a very rudimentary 'Schedule of Essential Repairs'.

He rang me that evening. "Dad says we should take his Foreman Geof up when we go next time to look over the barns. There isn't much that old Geof doesn't know how to fix." We decided we couldn't inflict our primitive camping conditions on this 60-year-old master craftsman, opting instead for a dawn departure, a high-speed tour of the site and then a brainstorming session in an upmarket quayside restaurant Brian knew down the coast at a place called Blakeney.

It was another depressingly miserable morning when we arrived at Stiffquay. I had yet to see the sun shine on the site. Sitting side-by-side on the van's bench seat we surveyed the bleak scene through the pickup's windscreen. Rain was being blown in diagonal gusts from the unfriendly North Sea. "Let's give it a minute or two to ease off, shall we?" Brian tactfully suggested. Geof rolled himself a cigarette. The 'minute' lasted half-an-hour.

Eventually we unlocked the padlocked five-bar gate and trudged through the mud up to the winnowing barn's entrance, which Brian unlocked, swinging the creaky doors back and chocking them with a couple of boulders. A clutch of pigeons flapped out, angrily complaining.

Brian unrolled his Schedule. "Geof: Nick and I need to take the dimensions of the cart shed next door and check its condition. So while we're doing that, mate, why don't you take a look at the winnowing barn's rear wall? Dad says its timber cladding is shot to pieces with woodworm and there's only a single bressummer beam supported on Acrow props, holding the whole thing up. He's classified it as 'extremely 'iffy'."

Geof gave a wry smile. "Right you be," he said, picking up his tool bag.

Brian fished a 100' steel measuring tape from his satchel and we set to, recording the cart shed's dimensions. "Dad says just insert a simple floor on softwood joists, with a staircase up to two bedrooms."

"And a bathroom?" I queried.

My new partner shook his head. "En suite washbasins are more economical…" but he never finished the sentence, as the earth shook with an almighty crash. "Quick! Next door!"

The winnowing barn was full of a choking dust. As it settled, we could make out the prone figure of Geof lying face-down in the dirt. One end of the beam which had supported the whole of the rear part of the barn lay on the ground only inches from Geof's head, while the rusty Acrow props lay in a clump of brambles. Brian cushioned the old craftsman's head with his satchel and took out a water flask to slake his thirst. He finally opened his eyes. "So, what happened, mate?" Brian asked.

The craftsman slowly shook his head in disbelief. "Search me, Brian. Gordon Bennett, I never touched them props. Honest. I saw they was all skew-nailed to the underside of the beam."

Brian looked at me quizzically and raised an eyebrow. He certainly wasn't going to hazard a guess as to how a 10" x 10" oak beam could fall and almost kill someone. It was a miracle that old Geof hadn't been despatched either by being crushed by the beam or stabbed through the head by a shard from the smashed pantiles that had rained down on him and now littered the ground all around. After about ten minutes and a thorough check that no bones had been broken we decided to call it a day.

But we continued with our plan to take a late lunch at The Blakeney Arms. It was a subdued affair, though the shaken old craftsman noticeably brightened when the waiter placed a large steak and kidney pie in front of him. And all three of us enjoyed a bottle of Cotes du Rhône. Beams and Acrow props were strictly 'off the menu'.

Our third foray to Stiffquay - this time without Geof - was to prove as eerie as the previous encounter.

With his father's help Brian had produced a very competent scaled floor plan of the winnowing barn and the adjoining cart shed. His sister Carol, who had recently been accepted as a student by the St Martin's School of Art in

London, had improved it immeasurably with some colour washes. With its beige carpeting and Conran furniture it looked quite habitable.

"Of course it's not costed, but since you're going to be a quantity surveyor one day, why don't you work out a 'ballpark' figure for a refurbishment?" Brian helpfully suggested. "That way we'll know whether it's worth putting in an offer." I agreed with the logic and that weekend set to work, though with slightly less enthusiasm since the incident of the fallen bressummer beam.

Carol wanted to accompany us on our next trip to Stiffquay. It was nearly Eastertime, considerably drier with daffodils lining the verges. As we pulled up, mid-morning shafts of angled sunlight lit up the old winnowing Barn, as if welcoming Carol. It seemed an altogether cheerier location.

While Brian and I logged all the dimensions of the old cart shed and its upper hay loft, Carol 'fine-tuned' her perspective of the barn's interior, with her colour-washed image stretched out on some boards laid on a trestle table. Suddenly she let out a piercing scream causing us to drop our tape and clip boards and dash to her rescue next door.

She was standing frozen in the opening to the barn's rear part, close to where Geof had had his lucky escape. The bressummer still lay where it had fallen a fortnight before. Attached to the end that pointed skywards was a taut length of orange fishing line. Threaded through the line was the body of a seagull, with its long white wings extended and its head hanging down forlornly. The bottom end of the line was attached to the handle of one of the Acrow props. Spread across Carol's watercolour drawing was a copy of the Kings Lynn estate agent's particulars, with the words 'NOT FOR SALE!' scrawled across it in blood red letters.

We couldn't wait to put as many miles as possible between us and creepy Norfolk.

12

The Romantic Dean

'CATHEDRAL Close Gardens. Residents Only'. The Dean paused briefly to admire the new sign affixed to the side of the arched brick entrance. He nodded with satisfaction. His instructions to the signwriting company had been followed to the letter: gold lettering on a Trafalgar blue background (BS 20 D 45), emulating the signage throughout the Cathedral Estate. A retired Chelsea Flower Show designer had been commissioned to design a small walled garden, created from a former storage yard for the old stones that were dressed by masons carrying out repairs to the historic cathedral's fabric.

He pushed open the wrought iron entrance gate. Early spring flowers were cautiously emerging beside a weeping willow which bowed low over a pool, fed from a U-shaped stone spout set in the wall. A right-angled two-storey block of 12 balconied retirement apartments formed the backdrop to Cathedral Close Gardens. Once again he smiled: all the Dean's idea. He paused to admire the way in which the carefully-created new garden seemed to have established itself in just three months.

A blonde middle-aged woman, slim and trimly attired in a pale blue dress, was seated on a wooden bench reading a book. From its crimson dust-jacket the Dean could see that it was Robert Harris' best-seller *Conclave*. The woman looked up and smiled. He hastily re-classified her age as late-40s.

"Apologies, madame, I didn't mean to disturb you." She marked the place in her novel, closed it and placed it beside her on the bench.

"I thought for a moment you were going to point out to me that this garden is only for the use of residents."

"Heaven forfend!"

"Because – you see – I *am* a resident." She gave a girlish giggle. "In fact, for my sins, I 'ave already been elected Secretary of the Residents Association!" He noted the dropped 'h' and her slightly foreign pronunciation of 'association'.

Smiling, he cautiously took a seat beside her on the bench. "So you're the new Secretary? And are your duties onerous?"

She made a 'fluttering' motion with a well-manicured hand. "*Comme ci, comme ça.*"

"I'm sure you are doing a splendid job." After a pause he asked: "And do you like it here?"

"I *love* it! The peaceful ambience… the solitude." She swept her arms sideways as if to encompass the entire walled garden. "Was it, may I ask, all your idea?"

"All what? The retirement apartments?"

"No, no. This peaceful garden."

He clenched his hands gently together as if in prayer, looked down at them and paused before answering. "Yes… yes, I suppose it was. With some Heavenly guidance." She placed a hand gently on his. "*C'est mervieux.*" The Dean blushed.

Two minutes of silence passed, disturbed only by the water spout behind them. Then consulting his watch he stood up. "I fear I must take my leave. It was a pleasure talking with you madame…"

"Mademoiselle, Dean."

"My apologies." He bowed and left the garden and headed for his weekly Meeting of Canons. The meeting dragged on interminably but little was achieved. All the

Dean could think of was his chance encounter with the attractive French woman.

Their second meeting in the walled garden was to be exactly a week later. Neither was naïve enough to believe that it was an accident. Wearing a pale yellow dress, she was once again engrossed in her copy of *Conclave*, though to judge from the number of unread pages, she was now close to the novel's dramatic denouement. "So, tell me, how are you getting on with Mr Harris's exciting story of the Papal Election?" he asked as he took a seat beside her.

"*Conclave*? I can't put it down, Dean! Last night I read until 1.00am! Do tell me: how many ballots are held?" He showed her the four fingers of both hands.

"EIGHT? *Mon Dieux*! I don't think I can bear the suspense!"

He knew time was short (yet another meeting of the Canons beckoned) and wanted to use every moment getting to know this attractive woman better. "So, what brought you to England, may I ask?"

She shrugged. "An affair of the heart, Dean. I was on the stage."

"An actress?"

"Sadly no. Merely a dancer."

"In Paris?"

"No, Marseille. He left me for a younger woman. From the same chorus line, would you believe?"

"Well, all I can say is that Tollminster's gain is Marseille's loss."

She blushed. "That is most kind."

The Dean consulted his watch. "Sadly, I must now go to take my weekly Meeting of the Canons – though I would much prefer to remain here talking to you…"

"Madeleine."

"Madeleine? My favourite place of worship in all Paris!" he told her bashfully as he rose. "I will say *adieu*."

Two days later the Dean found a hand-delivered letter on his office desk. 'Would you do me the kindness of joining me for tea this afternoon – shall we say around 4.00 pm?' It was initialled 'M'.

The Dean nervously climbed the stairs of the apartment block and walked along the polished woodblock landing until he had located the apartment address on the top of the invitation he had received that morning. Madeleine answered the door chime promptly. She was wearing a patterned semi-diaphanous pink housecoat and her hair was tied with a pink bow. He wondered whether he should now 'reclassify' his guesstimate of her age yet again. "Do please come in, Dean," she invited sweetly. As he slipped past her in the narrow passageway, he couldn't fail to notice her Chanel perfume.

She had left the apartment's doors onto the balcony ajar, causing the net curtains to billow up, enticing in the spring fragrances of the walled garden below. The tea was also a delight: Earl Grey, served in bone china teacups, with *mille-feuille* pastries. "A little attempt at *entente cordiale*" was his hostess's whispered explanation.

"Our garden, or rather I should say 'your' garden, Madeleine, has been entered for an award at this year's Chelsea Flower Show. Are you, I wonder, familiar with the event?"

"No, I'm afraid not, Dean."

"It's a great English horticultural occasion. The Cathedral is always invited to the official Royal opening, though sadly the Bishop invariably intercepts our invitation and takes his wife. Perhaps…" he paused before the indiscretion "…I should try to way-lay it this year and take you!"

Madeleine clasped her hands and blushed. "That would be… *merveilleux* Dean!"

It was gone 1.00 am when the Cathedral's most senior cleric returned to his house. Ignoring the cold supper which had been left for him by his housekeeper he went straight to bed.

No obvious excuse presented itself in the following days to revisit Cathedral Close Gardens and, frustratingly, inclement weather curtailed any daytime strolls. On the third day the Dean had to travel by train to London to attend a meeting at Church House, Westminster, at the behest of the Bishop (the subject: 'Accelerating Female Ordination'). 'Such a tiresome topic' was his superior's snap verdict. 'Next thing you know it'll be LGBTQ!' He returned late in the evening on the last train.

He could contain his emotions no longer, whatever the weather. The following morning, sporting a heavy waterproof coat, he strode out through the rain.

Parked across the entrance to Cathedral Close he was surprised to encounter a large half-filled furniture pantechnicon, with all its contents discreetly covered by dust sheets. Three removal men were inside the van having a tea break, seated on the same floral sofa the Dean had taken tea on less than a week before. The foreman eyed the dark-clothed stranger, nodded at him respectfully and announced: "The foreign lady's jist gorn down Marks & Spencer, your reverence." The Dean flounced off.

He returned to the sanctity of his office in the Cloisters to retrieve the handwritten invitation card to tea which Madeleine had sent him, but it showed no mobile phone number. Amongst the pile of mail and minutes which had been left on his desk was the Cathedral's internal newsletter. Headed CATHEDRAL CLOSE, a boxed item at the bottom read: 'A vacancy has unexpectedly arisen in our new block of retirement apartments. Please contact the Cathedral Office if you know of any worshipper who might be interested'. The Dean lifted the internal 'phone which connected him directly with the Bishop. After giving a brief resumé of his exhausting trip to London he asked about Madeleine's surprise departure.

"The Secretary of the Residents Association, you mean?" the Bishop asked gruffly. "That French woman?"

"Yes, I believe so, Bishop."

"*'Faire le trottoir'* is the French colloquial description for her trade, so I'm told."

"Meaning?"

"Come, come Dean; what happened to your schoolboy French? 'Working the pavement' is I believe the literal translation!"

13

No Pets Allowed

"ANDREW? It's Anita!"

He was just making his second espresso. Still in his pyjamas and undecided about how the day might pan out. A walk through the park down to Soho seemed a likely option.

"Hi there, Anita. Long time no speak. Where've you been?"

"Working, darling. You know – the same old, same old."

"But you're supposed to be retired!"

"Try telling that to He Who Shall Be Obeyed."

He sipped the coffee and smiled. Bubbly as ever, even at 8.00 am. And she'd lost none of her wit.

"So, what's on your agenda for this glorious Saturday, sweetie?" she coyly enquired.

"Well… once I'm dressed and Rudy has had his morning constitutional, I thought I'd walk through the park down to Soho and do a bit of shopping. Maybe visit one or two of our old haunts."

"Wish I was coming too."

"Same here. *Patisserie Valerie* will definitely be on the list." There was a pause on the line as they each recalled fond memories of Soho's legendary French café. "A bit of food shopping, then I'll go to Jimmy the Greek's for lunch. Then this afternoon I intend to start constructing one of my famous seafood *paellas* (remember them?). I've got two old friends coming for supper."

"Maybe I should come and join you; make it a cosy qartet?"

"If only!"

"Who are they – your supper guests?"

"BBC Desmond and Polish Andy."

"Best Man at our wedding!"

"The same."

"And how is Andy – still effortlessly suave?"

"Natch."

"Well, I must say you seem to be coping OK."

"You mean without you?"

"Yeah… I suppose so."

"I have good days and bad days, Anita. Today looks like being one of the better ones – probably as a result of this call. How about you?"

"The same, I guess. Though our circumstances are somewhat different!"

He finished his coffee. "Don't remind me. By the way Dr Phelps has put me on a new drugs regime."

"And?"

"Says we won't be able to measure its effectiveness for four to six weeks."

"Charming! D'you trust him?"

"No more than any other shrink."

After a moment's reflection: "I should give it a go Andrew. Those six weeks will probably fly by."

He walked over to the window and surveyed the sunlit park, which was still comparatively quiet. "I'm not so sure. Workwise things are pretty iffy at the moment. There's even talk of voluntary redundancies."

"How come?"

"Seems we lost a big hotel commission to an Arab conglomerate. And if it's 'last in, first out', which is how they tackled it last time, it'll be yours truly for the chop."

Walking back to the apartment's kitchen area he swung the fridge door open to remove a bottle of wine. Hearing the clink of ice cubes in a glass the caller asked: "Bit early to be drinking, isn't it sweetie?"

"It's never too early to savour New Zealand's wonderful Cloudy Bay elixir, Anita!"

"Even so, Andrew, I should go steady – especially if you're already dosed up with Dr Phelps' 'little helpers'!"

"Yeah, I suppose you're right. Listen, it was lovely hearing from you again. Please don't leave it so long next time."

"It isn't easy calling from here, you know."

"What are you working on?"

"We're overdubbing an old German film by Wim Wenders. You might know it: *Wings of Desire*."

"Wow! One of my all-time favourites. Black-and-white. Shot in Berlin."

"That's the one!"

"Peter Falk is rubbish."

"Tell me about it." She began a fit of giggles. "We've been wracking our brains how we might 'excise' all his scenes!" Then, after a pause: "So what would be your other favourites if the BFI ran a 'Macabre Movies' season?"

"Well, here's one you probably haven't run into: Anthony Minghella's *Truly. Madly. Deeply.*"

Anita shrieked with delight. "With Juliet Stevenson? Black and white again. It won her a BAFTA. I love it to pieces!"

There was a moment's pause on the line, then the silence was filled with the slow haunting notes of the Bach cello solo which ends the film.

"How ever did you do that, Nita?"

"It's called Celestial Technology, darling!"

"Hey - here's one you'll probably remember – you took me to the Premier: *A Matter of Life and Death*."

"David Niven and Kim Hunter? My first job as a Props Store Gofer. 'Anita: Gofer 8 portions of cod and chips, darling!'"

"Nevertheless, you survived."

"Michael Powell was a real gentleman, but Emeric Pressburger was too melodramatic for my liking. Hungarian. Invariably got his way."

"Like making you locate London's longest escalator. Where was it you found it?"

"Holborn Underground. It all had to be shot at night after the Tube closed down. And switching from technicolour to black and white, with that moody music, made it seem really eerie." She giggled and lightened up. "Take my word for it, darling: it's not a bit like that!"

Andrew poured himself a second glass of wine. As if resigned to the fact that he would never see the Park, Andrew's *dachshund* crawled under the sofa into his basket.

"Still there?"

"Yup. You OK for time?"

"Yup. Rudy's out for the count."

Another giggle cascaded down the line. "And I shouldn't think it will be too long before his master will be zonked as well!"

"Why can't we have more conversations like this? You can't imagine how good it is to hear your voice again."

"I know sweetie: but 'rules is rules', as they never cease reminding us up here. No incoming calls."

"Not even emergencies?"

"Nope."

"Is there any way at all that you can think of, darling, that we could meet up again?"

After a long pause, she came back, quietly and plaintively. "Meet again? Only one way I know of, Andrew. And it's not going to be one your Dr Phelps would approve of."

"And that is?"

"The 'route' I decided to take a year ago."

"Go on."

"Down the hall corridor to the cloakroom by the front door. Medicine cabinet. Top shelf. Extreme left. The bottle's marked 'Paracetamol'".

He placed his empty wine glass on the window sill and gazed out at the park. "Can I bring Rudy?"

"'Fraid not, sweetie. No Pets Allowed."

14

Their First Customer

GLANCING through the shop window the man could discern precious little activity. It was, after all, only just after 8.30 am with office workers streaming out of the Underground station opposite. Then he caught sight of the unmistakable illuminated profile of a gleaming Italian Gaggia coffee machine. He tried the front door – and it opened! He was greeted with an enticing smell of freshly-baked biscuits.

"Good morning," he asked nervously, "are you open?"

"But of course, monsieur. In fact, you are our first customer!" a diminutive middle-aged lady in a crisp pinafore called from behind the counter. "Please to come in." Moments later she cautiously approached the man's table, order pad extended. She noticed he was smartly dressed.

"I was admiring your wonderful Gaggia espresso machine through the shop window," he opened, to make polite conversation. "D'you suppose it could make me a double *macchiato*?"

She scribbled something on her pad. "I think I'd better ask my husband. It was he who was given the demonstration by the Gaggia people when they came to install it earlier this week." She scurried away, then returned with a small plate of heart-shaped shortbread biscuits and a glass of water. 'All very Italian,' the man thought.

The waitress's bespectacled partner nervously emerged from the back kitchens and the Gaggia soon burst into life with hissing steam sounds and glowing blue lights illuminating its front panel. Handles were raised and lowered. Three minutes later, without speaking, the operator placed a small dark blue china cup and saucer in front of the solitary customer, nodded and retreated to his kitchen.

The *macchiato* was perfect, its tiny blob of frothed milk lightly dusted with chocolate powder.

The customer glanced around the premises. It had obviously been a café before. The unmarked cream laminate tabletops were covered by crisp white tablecloths, with a small glass vase on each table containing a sprig of white snowdrops. Seating was scarlet-coloured, cane-seated Thonet chairs, all in remarkably good condition. The tomato-shaped ketchup containers were the only undisguised sign that this had formerly been a working man's 'caf', though it seemed to the stranger that the new owners intended to bring it up in the world.

Beyond the open doorway the brightly-lit kitchen looked spotless. Above the bar the new owners had hung a print of Manet's famous Impressionist classic *A Bar at the Folie Bergerè*. 'Good luck to this plucky couple' the man thought to himself, as the waitress returned.

"And how was your coffee, monsieur?" she asked nervously.

"Ten-out-of-ten! If I'd closed my eyes, I could have been in Bologna!"

Standing in the open doorway, the waitress's partner smiled with satisfaction. "May I make you another, monsieur?" he asked.

The customer held up the palms of his hands in mock-supplication. "I'm afraid my caffeine count couldn't cope, excellent though it was. But thank you nevertheless." He nibbled a shortbread biscuit.

As the café wasn't busy and the man still had time to kill before his 9.30 am appointment, he ventured to extend his conversation with the cautious couple. "So, what brought you to this area of London?" he asked.

She looked to her partner to answer. "I had an old-established tobacconist's business in the City in Chancery Lane, sir. Glashan's. We were only tenants."

"I know it well", said the stranger.

"The freehold changed hands. And our new landlord turned out to be a Russian oligarch – if that isn't a racially-derogatory term to use these days. He had ideas which were way beyond our means. So, when the time came to renew our lease we gave in our notice. And Emily found us this little café."

"And do you judge Bermondsey to be on the up-and-up?"

The proprietor looked to his partner to answer. "*New* Bermondsey, sir! Yes, very much so. That racket you can hear is the excavations for a tower block of flats – 75 per cent of which are to be 'affordable'. 'Barely-affordable' is probably nearer the mark" the man added wryly.

"The MP Robert Jenerick came and laid the foundation stone only last week. We will probably be the builders' first port of call – it's to be a Dutch construction company," the waitress told him. "Then hopefully the tenants and their families will come, when they move in. This place should see us comfortably into old age."

"The one 'ingredient' that we are still missing is an eye-catching name," the man said. And the signwriter is coming on Friday to paint the fascia! Gaggia have told us that they'll even return to replicate our chosen name on the front." He fondly patted the side of his treasured Italian machine.

The customer looked down at his cup. "Perhaps I will have another *macchiato* after all – but only a single, if you please."

The man switched on some controls and turned the knob of the steam outlet. "Certainly sir."

"Right, so what will be the main 'fare' you'll be offering – apart from excellent coffees?" the customer asked the couple.

The lady spoke first: "Freshly-made sandwiches on open *brochette* bread with healthy vegetable-based fillings." Then her husband added: "Plus Emily's speciality: chocolate-based cakes and confectionery. Our son Simon has just been accepted as a mature student in the factory of the famous Belgian chocolatiers Galler in Liège." he added proudly.

"I know their champagne truffles well," the new customer reminisced with a smile. The proprietor handed the fresh coffee to his wife, who brought it to the stranger's table. He took another biscuit.

On finishing his coffee, the man looked at his watch. "Sadly, I must depart. May I have my bill?"

The couple looked at each other and nodded. "As you are our very first customer, monsieur, consider the coffees 'on the house'".

Their visitor took his wallet from an inside pocket, slipped out a banknote by way of a tip and scribbled something on the back of a visiting card. He handed the man the banknote folded around his card. "That is most generous. I am a solicitor, so feel free to call me if there are any little legal problems troubling you. Inside, I've scribbled a suggestion for you to show your signwriter on Friday. It seems to me that you need a name which will resound across the community, signalling to young and old alike your appreciation of chocolate. My thanks for a most enjoyable visit. And good luck!"

Only after the stranger had departed, heading for the Underground station, did the man unfold the note. He read the reverse of the card, smiled, and showed it to his wife.

In an elegant script the lawyer had written: 'Wonka's'.

15

Paradise Lost

"SO you're the Limey, are you?" Tim studied his inquisitor: a muscular crew-cut man in his early 30s, wearing a checked shirt and bleached jeans. The chance encounter was in a crowded bar in Chico, California. Piped country-and-western music made long conversations almost impossible.

"That's me. Tim from Birmingham."

"Birmingham Alabama?"

"Nope. Birmingham, West Midlands."

"So whatcha-all do back in Birmingham-west-midlands, Tim?"

"I'm a quantity surveyor. I work in the construction industry. You?"

"Forestry. And I'm an auxiliary firefighter."

Through gentle – and not-so-gentle – elbowing they managed to make their way to the edge of the bar counter. Steve held up two fingers and called to the barman "Buds!"

They beat a hasty retreat to the bar's outside terrace, where the decibel count was just as loud but the ambient temperature was about 20 degrees cooler than in the smoky interior.

"So where are you headed next?" the forester asked.

"Nowhere special. I'd love to walk in Yosemite but I haven't got time. My flight back to England's on Friday. But I'd like to see more of this state; possibly even get up to Oregon."

"And how'll you get there?" Steve asked.

"Oh, I dunno; Greyhound, I guess."

"There's a much better way, my friend," the forester told him, up-ending the dregs of his Budweiser. "It's faster, with epic scenic vistas. And it's free!"

"Really? How come?" the startled English tourist asked.

"Why, you jump a train. Like the hobos do. I'll come with you if you like." Steve then gave the Englishman 'edited highlights' of the art of illegally boarding a freight train in the state's main marshalling yard, prior to being transported north to Oregon, free of charge. "Takes about six hours," he concluded. "So, would you up for it, Tim?"

"Not half!"

Tim and Steve met up next the following evening in the boondocks of Sacramento's sprawling freight yards. It was dusk, at the end of a blisteringly hot summer's day.

Slipping through a giant gash in the yard's wire security fence the two men headed towards the orange glow of a campfire, around which about twenty shabbily clad vagrants were huddled. Several showed severed arm stumps below their shirt sleeves. Two had partially-amputated legs.

A swarthy Mexican (wearing a chef's hat) appeared to be in charge of the cooking arrangements. "Leave me to chat to these guys," Tim was relieved to be told by his guide. Minutes later the Chef indicated them to join the group, handing Steve a tin plate on which were two perfectly prepared stuffed tortillas.

"Pablo, over there…" Steve nodded across the fire – "says there's an Oregon-bound freighter out of here at midnight. How does that sound?"

"Fine by me," the Englishman acquiesced, still really none the wiser as to what he'd agreed. Handing him the platter, Tim's mentor and guide sprung up. "Right. You stay here; I'll go and reserve us a couple of seats."

'How terribly civilised' Tim thought. 'Free admission to a barbecue; and now my American travelling companion has gone off to reserve our seats! Network Rail certainly needs to up its game!'

Half-an-hour later the two friends were nervously sculking alongside the parked Oregon-bound freighter. It seemed to stretch to infinity: boxcars, tankers and countless double-decked automobile carriers, each wagon neatly labelled with its destination. Every so often the line of freight cars would 'shudder' as another carriage was attached at the rear.

"Boxcars are out tonight, buddy," Steve whispered back to his companion. "All the best seats in the house are already gone! There's an unwritten rule that the 'regular travellers' don't like 'sharing'." With which the leviathan made an ominous shudder, setting off multiple clanking 'complaints' from the stationery carriages' steel buffers. "Right, follow me!"

Steve quickly climbed the fixed steel ladder of a two-level vehicle transporter. Tim needed no second command and followed. At the top the two trespassers slipped noiselessly into the spacious upholstered cab of a pristine Mitsubishi pickup truck. And just as Steve carefully swung the door quietly shut, the metallic squeaks from below indicated that their night freight express to Oregon was pulling out of the Sacramento freight yards. The dashboard clock showed a few minutes after midnight.

The freighter settled into a steady pace of around 40 mph once it had cleared the marshalling yards and Sacramento's suburbs. "Take a nap if you want, buddy," Steve suggested.

"No fear! This is all too good to miss."

"D'you know how many miles of working rail track there is out there?"

"Tell me."

"100,000 route miles. All well maintained." Tim was too ashamed to admit to the UK's paltry 21,000 total and hoped that his guide had never heard of Dr Beeching.

"Up ahead shortly, when we cross into Northern California, I'll show you the scene of the largest firefight I ever experienced. Lost three of my buddies."

A near-full moon illuminated a heavily forested area. Suddenly, on the left-hand side, Tim perceived a weird denuded landscape, its only standing trees being black-scarred totem-like stumps which cast eerie shadows over the blackened soil.

"Whatever is that?"

"That, my friend, was the self-built community of Paradise, started by some hippies up from Haight-Ashbury back in the 70s. It covered nearly 100 acres."

"So what happened?"

"Seems a heavy-duty overhead power line was blown down in the night by a freak storm. Sparks from the severed cable ignited pine tinder – it hadn't rained for weeks – and the fire just rushed through the community. Most of the permanent dwellings were only timber-framed and there were loads of other folk living in caravans or campervans. Even yurts. When we arrived up from Chico, there was a traffic jam of folk escaping back to 'Frisco of more than 1,000 vehicles!"

"Was there anything left that could be salvaged?"

"Nope. Not a thing." With which Steve fell silent, next brightening up half-an-hour later with the alarming news that their jumping off point was 'up ahead, around about a couple of miles'.

"How will we know?"

"Don't worry, buddy, I've done this before. There's a huge sawmill that works around the clock, all floodlit at night. You can't miss it!"

"And that's where we bale out?"

"You got it! You'll go first. Hitch all your belongings around your neck, climb down the steel ladder fixed to the side of the wagon we came up by. Count up to eight rungs. Repeat please?"

"I'm to descend eight rungs on the fixed steel ladder."

"Correct. Then with both arms laced through the ladder's uprights you have to turn through 180 degrees…"

"So I'm facing outwards?"

"You got it!"

"Then?"

"Then you jump, boyo – step into space. But remember: you jump OUTWARDS. Not back – unless you want to lose a leg like some of those hobos back in Sacramento. Be sure to roll away from the passing freight cars' wheels. If we're lucky, we should hit level clinkered ground – though there are one or two embankments, so you might find yourself rolling downhill! Play possum 'til I come along. And let's hope there's no cattle in the field."

At 40 mph Tim's ladder descent was frightening. Executing the 180 degree turn, with the cacophony of the nearby steel buffers adding to the tension, was almost more than he could bear. As he froze stock still, facing outwards, he caught sight through the blackness of the sawmill's illuminated profile: a huge green corrugated tower as tall as Big Ben. Closing his eyes he stepped into the blackness.

Tim lay rigidly still on the clinker, deafened by the sound of the passing wheels. He cautiously moved his limbs and was relieved to find no bones broken. Ten minutes later he was joined by his cheerful travelling companion and guide.

"The highway's about a quarter mile dead ahead. Then all we gotta do is hitch a lift south. If we're lucky there might even be an all-night bar where we can have waffles for breakfast."

"And please," Tim implored "can we wash them down with a large Jack Daniels?"

16

Queens of the Silver Screen

FROM Gabor to Gardner, Harlow to Hepburn and Mansfield to Monroe. Then there was also Bacall and Garbo, Russell and Taylor. There was room in Heaven for all of them. And hadn't they all staked out a delightfully exclusive preserve for themselves?

I was a mere *sommelier* (one notch up from a waiter, but light years away from ever being selected as a *maître d'hôtel*,) but I loved my job and always appreciated the compliments I received from these wonderful Queens of the Silver Screen.

It was a privileged job in beautiful surroundings. The silk-draped walls of our marble hall seemed to stretch to infinity; there was always acres of dazzling sunshine streaming in through the stained glass windows at the farthest end; the highly polished cream terrazzo floor was lined with a profusion of oriental rugs from China to Kazakhstan; and there were stylish Louis Quinze silk-upholstered armchairs and sofas galore. There were flowers everywhere - Miss Hepburn and Miss Gardner being especially fond of gardenias – and cooing doves nested at the very top of some of the Great Hall's marble columns.

Breakfast merged seamlessly into elevenses; lunch took most of the afternoon (until it was teatime) and dinner invariably lasted until bedtime. Throughout the day, vintage Moët was available 'on tap'. "Randall?" Miss Monroe would often whisper to me as I passed - "Could you'all just fix me one more glass of fizzy - as a nightcap please, sweetie?" JFK would sometimes put in a discreet appearance – usually sitting in the shadow of one of the marble columns – if there was a whisper that Miss Monroe was going to do her famous ukulele number from *Some Like it Hot*.

Entertainment was provided for the ladies by countless visiting musicians and singers, with the principal accolades being shared between Billie Holiday (her torch songs were always especially moving) and the full Benny Goodman Orchestra. On a good night the entire ensemble would leave the stage for a 10-minute 'ciggy break' whenever Gene Krupa began his *Sing, Sing, Sing* drum solo. Another legendary torch singer was Miss Marlene Dietrich. Back-kitchen gossip had it that Miss Dietrich 'had the hots' for Miss Garbo.

Gentlemen visitors were admitted at the sole discretion of the *Maitre d'Hotel,* Monsieur Charles, formerly of The Ritz Hotel in London. Two of our regular diners were Charles Boyer (Miss Hepburn invariably had to restrain him from bursting into song at the dinner table) and debonair Errol Flynn, who on one embarrassing occasion turned up in his *Robin Hood* costume, including those figure-hugging forest green tights! Much to Miss Bacall's chagrin, taciturn Mr Bogart invariably declined all dinner invitations. Bogart and Kennedy were like two peas from the same pod. Emotionally fixated by Bacall and Monroe, but publicly always distantly aloof.

After a quiet dinner one evening, Miss Zsa Zsa, in her role as the party's most senior figure (by virtue of both her age and her nine husbands) raised the question of enlarging the group. Word had come from Central Admin that a number of applications had been made to join the exclusive Queens of the Silver Screen group, though I personally felt that 10 was a nice tidy number. In the kitchens, the rumour was that Princess Grace of Monaco – née Miss Grace Kelly – had headed the waiting list for at least two decades! Also, the English Princess Margaret was said to be getting very impatient and, when a Heavenly official queried her 'connections' with the cinema, was angrily told: "I've been on almost as many world newsreels as my sister!"

As the port decanter was circulated, a slightly tipsy Miss Monroe vouchsafed that Miss Kelly would be more than welcome – "just so long as she's not allowed to bring that perv Hitch along as her guest." The general murmur of agreement around the table seemed to indicate that others had had unfortunate encounters with the esteemed English film director, or "that Leytonstone *parvenu*" as Miss Bacall tartly put it. *Parvenu* I knew (Monsieur Charles would often use it about lazy kitchen hands) but Leytonstone was new to me. The normally placid Miss Hepburn recalled poor Tippi Hedren's brave ordeal against those marauding gulls in the film *The Birds*. And the old buzzard didn't exactly give Miss Kelly an easy ride in *Dial M for Murder* if you remember! In the end, the matter of enlarging the group was adjourned and I was instructed to break the news to the two princesses.

At weekends, when we couldn't book a big band, some of my ladies would provide the musical entertainment for themselves. Miss Monroe, Miss Russell and Miss Bacall often performed that show-stopping number from their film *How to Marry a Millionaire*, with Miss Monroe reprising her *Running Wild* ukulele solo as an encore (she never failed to turn up without that hip flask tucked into her stocking top!). In the absence of Tony Curtis and Jack Lemmon, saxophone and bass accompaniment usually came from Stan Getz and Charles Mingus.

Miss Russell would occasionally regale us with details of her on-off dalliances with the reclusive Howard Hughes, who not only created the world's largest flying boat (the *Spruce Goose*), but also designed a special 'up-lift' bra for her to wear in that notorious hay barn scene in the movie

The Outlaw. "It was full of darned girders," she recalled. "In the end I just screwed up some Kleenex tissues."

With enough Oscars and other awards between them to sink the *Bismarck*, my ladies were never backward at coming forward when it came to drama. Or melodrama. By far and away my favourite re-enactment – featuring the film's two original screen actors – was the final scene from *Queen Christina*, which many film lovers regard as Miss Garbo's greatest screen performance. Knowing I had a soft spot for her, she had once graciously presented me with an autographed photograph of herself, sitting forlornly on the deck of the *Queen Mary* liner as it approached New York harbour. She is shown surrounded by hat boxes (at least eight) but no helpers, or aides. She looks thoroughly miserable and the photo immediately conjures up her famous 'I want to be alone' remark. In our Heavenly Marble Hall she was shy but always courteous.

In *Queen Christina* (if you've never seen it) Miss Garbo plays an unmarried 17th century Swedish Queen, while the suave matinée idol John Gilbert (at that time her lover, pipping Laurence Olivier to the post for the starring role) is cast as a Spanish diplomat who falls head over heels in love with her, after a bedroom seduction scene that would never have been passed by the Hays Office had it then existed! Though there is minimal dialogue (which suited Miss Garbo) the couple's body language says it all.

The film's poignant ending – Gilbert has been fatally wounded in a sword fight – leaves a grieving Christina, hunched up like a mute figurehead, on the prow of her royal sailing barge which is to take her back to her Palace in Stockholm. Her sombre pose reminded me of the treasured photograph I had in my locker. And when I say there wasn't a dry eye in our marble hall that night, I'm not exaggerating.

17

Venice

THE Dean's enforced leave of absence, following the misunderstanding (on the part of the Bishop) over the former's motives in befriending the exotic French lady who had briefly occupied one of the Cathedral's new retirement apartments, came as a merciful relief. Venice beckoned.

Financed by a clutch of redeemed ISAs which he had long wanted to put to good use before his retirement, the worthy cleric booked himself a berth on the famed *Orient Express* to Venice. It was to be a 7-day round trip, with accommodation in the city not in one of the notoriously expensive hotels beside the Grand Canal, but in an unfashionable Air b'n'b garret, tucked away behind the Rialto Market. It had been tracked down for him by an internet-savvy chorister.

Burdened only be light carry-on luggage the Dean joined the *Venice Simplon* in good time at Victoria Station. The single compartment, with an adjoining minuscule washroom and toilet, was adequate, with its panelled walls lined with enticing photos of the landscape which the train was to pass through on its 700-mile journey to the famed La Serenissima.

His afternoon studies were interrupted by a tap on the compartment's door. He leaned across from his sofa-bed and opened it to reveal a tall uniformed female ticket collector clutching a document file. She wore a crisp dark blue uniform, a maroon peaked cap and a lapel badge identifying her as EVA.

"Your reservation tickets and passport, monsieur?" she asked politely. The Dean rummaged in the wallet the travel agency had given him and handed them to the young woman. She quickly checked through them and handed them back with a smile. "Thank you, monsieur. Everything is in order. And for your dinner tonight, monsieur?" she enquired. "Would you like the first or the second sitting?"

"The second, if I may mademoiselle. That way I will be able to sit here and see the outskirts of Paris before it is dark."

She gave a little smile and ticked a box on her clipboard. "Quite so. You will be seated in the Lalique Salon, which is the furthest carriage."

"Lalique? *The* Lalique?" queried the Dean.

"*Bien sur, monsieur.* The engraved glass wall panels you will be sitting beneath came from the Paris workshops of Réne Lalique. Your dinner will be served at 9.00 pm." Tipping the peak of her cap coquettishly, she smiled at the Dean and departed.

The dinner surpassed all his expectations. A prawn cocktail, followed by coq au vin, with a mouth-watering crème brulé for dessert. All washed down by a half-bottle of Pouilly-Fumé from the Loire Valley. While the waiters discreetly cleared places and served coffee, the tinkling sounds of a grand piano drifted down from the adjoining salon. As he prepared to return to his compartment the Dean looked up, to be greeted by the attractive young ticket inspector. Sadly, she didn't linger.

"Just one more carriage, then I'm turning in." She gave him a cheeky wink. "*Dormez bien!*"

Bright and early the following morning, epic Alpine vistas were followed by lush green plains as the Venice Simplon navigated its way down towards La Serenissima and the perilously fragile timber crossing that would take the train across the lagoon onto the island.

Ranged along its arrival platform to bid farewell to the departing passengers were the entire crew of the *Orient Express*, including coquettish Eva who smiled sweetly at the Dean.

Stepping outside into the dazzling early morning sunshine, the Dean was confronted by a scene straight from a Canaletto, with the palazzo-lined Grand Canal full to the brim with gondolas and sleek motor launch taxis. The Dean knew that his Rialto destination was only three stops along the canal and opted for a crowded *vaporetto*. He alighted after it had passed under the famous 'arched' bridge and strolled through the bustling Rialto Market.

The directions to his accommodation supplied by his Venetian 'hosts' couldn't have been easier. Without being distracted by all the market's wonderful fresh fruit and vegetables on offer, he followed the proscribed route that eventually took him to a low brick archway and the narrow staircase leading up to his garret. Three steep wooden flights concluded before an iron-studded planked door. And beneath its threadbare doormat was the front door key!

It hardly qualified for the description 'Apartment' (the chorister had already warned him of that). More 'A Room with a View'. But what a view. There, centre stage across the Grand Canal, was the majestic 15th century basilica of San Zanipolo. He dropped his bags and gripped the window frame of the opened window in awe. After several minutes of reflection and prayer, the Dean turned around to assess his minuscule 'bolthole'. The Kelim-covered sofa clearly doubled as his bed for the night; the small pine table was to serve as a dining table for one; and a galley-style space beyond was obviously the kitchen.

His hosts had left him a bottle of wine, with a welcome card written in Italian and he was just about to commence a search for a corkscrew when he heard a faint tap on the door. He cautiously swung it open, expecting to be confronted by some shawl-wearing local crone checking him out. Instead, it was Eva, the smiling young ticket collector from the *Orient Express* – now capless, with lovely tresses of auburn hair framing her oval face. *"Buongiorno!"* Lovingly cradled in her arm was a bottle of Prosecco and from her wrist hung a small straw basket of green and black olives. The Dean was dumb-struck.

"Well, aren't you going to invite me in?" she asked in that same coquettish manner she'd employed when they first met on the train.

The Dean blushed. "Humble apologies. Please forgive me, dear lady." He beckoned her to enter.

Two glasses were found in the galley, the sparkling wine was uncorked, and framed by the garret's sole outside window, the Dean and the ticket collector raised their glasses to toast the shimmering basilica. Half-an-hour (and half a bottle) later they were seated side-by-side on the sofa bed. "D'you like pizza? I mean genuine home-cooked Italian pizza?" she asked.

"Can't say I've ever had one," the Dean meekly admitted. "Tollminster's pizzerias are all mere franchises."

She kicked off her pumps and topped up their glasses. "Right. There's a square not a hundred metres from your front door whose oven-cooked pizzas are famed throughout Venice. Would you like me to show you where it is?"

"By all means. Just so long as we can make the evening service at the Basilica first."

"But of course."

"How will we get there?"

"How do you get anywhere in Venice, honey? By water taxi!"

The service – an extended version of the English evensong – didn't end until nearly 8.00 pm, by which time it was dark. The Dean and Eva opted to return to the Rialto by motor launch, collecting their pre-ordered supper from the corner shop near the Dean's garret.

"So, when do you have to make the return trip?" he asked nervously, having put off the question all afternoon.

"Monday morning. The train leaves promptly at 8.00 am but the train crew has to be aboard by 7," she said cheerily, carrying in two warmed up orange and red pepper tarts from the little galley. She cheekily 'tweaked' his cheek with her fingers. "Why so glum?"

"Well, I suppose because it means we've only got one more day together," he replied glumly.

"Yes, but we've also got two whole nights!"

18

Mirage

I WAS recovering from a nasty Covid infection (my second) and my GP had recommended a 'healthy holiday, somewhere warm and relaxing, where you can take gentle daily exercise'. I knew Crete fitted the bill perfectly as I'd twice before visited the island. It was outside the busy school holiday season and so a week's stay in a small hotel just outside Heraklion was easy to organise. It was May, and the best time as far as climate and walking conditions were concerned.

After a couple of days spent by the hotel's pool I was itching to tackle an all-day excursion. It had long been my ambition to visit the famous Samariá Gorge. But at 16 kilometres (even though it is entirely downhill) I decided it might be a bit of a stretch. There would probably be mobs of tourists and giving up halfway through fatigue would present problems.

A helpful clerk on the hotel's reception desk said that the little-known Zakros Gorge would be a far better bet for me; it was 6km shorter than Samaria and terminated on a beach of the Libyan Sea, where there were boats in the late afternoon to ferry you back to Heraklion.

It was only after I'd asked him to make the booking that he added with a wry smile: "Zakros means 'valley of the dead', sir."

The minibus pick-up from the hotel was painless and with only a party of four Germans on board, all augured well that Zakros wouldn't be overrun with foreign tourists.

Half-an-hour later the driver set us down at the start point, indicating the way-marked route that would take us gently down to the coast. The hotel had provided an ample packed lunch and a litre flask of water and my trusty backpack had chocolate bars, binoculars and an all-weather anorak.

Within quarter-of-an-hour, by dawdling to admire the late-spring flowers, I'd let the German contingent go on ahead.

The sharp V-shaped vista directly ahead of me appeared as a twinkling azure ocean beneath a cloudless blue sky, framed by gaunt verdant-green craggy cliffs, inhabited only by birds. The athletic Germans were now mere pin-pricks.

I checked my watch, which indicated that I had just over four hours to stroll down to catch the ferry. Spotting a smooth rock outcrop up ahead, I decided to stop for a snack and a drink. In my trusty old ex-WD binoculars I could just pick up the tail end of the German quartet disappearing behind a cliff.

It was warming up nicely – approaching 20 degrees centigrade – and already the panoramic vista was beginning to shimmer gently. It was then that I spotted an unexpected movement across the valley floor, not far from the point where I'd last seen the German hikers.

A rather bedraggled group of around 20 dark-skinned males, all wearing pale loin cloths, was slowly crossing the valley floor in the direction of the cliffs opposite. Then a larger second group emerged, including women wearing brightly coloured shawls over their heads. Some carried infants, some dragged pushchairs loaded with clothes and provisions, while older children walked behind. Several of the women carried sealed white plastic packages, no bigger than laundry parcels.

Behind them were war-weary Asian refugees from Bangladesh and Myanmar, followed by a clutch of kippah-wearing rabbis carrying a banner marked 'Remember Auschwitz'. It was a desultory, solemn-looking collection.

Next, I heard the slow rhythmic beat of several djembe drums. Their male players appeared, flanking a contingent of battle-scarred refugees, many wearing dust- and debris-stained loin cloths. Two youths, bringing up the rear, carried a black, red and green Palestinian banner between them.

I swung my field glasses round in an effort to try to see where this procession might be headed. In a long fissure in the right-hand cliff face stood a magnificent pair of stone gateposts, easily a majestic match for the entrance gates that guard Buckingham Palace. They were surmounted by gilded horses, reminiscent of the famous horses of St Mark's Square in Venice.

From these gateposts hung a huge pair of pearlescent gates, with one leaf swung open and the other shut. And in front of the opening, clasping the side of the closed gate's ornamental ironwork, was a tall bearded figure holding a gold key. He was dressed entirely in white. The head of the procession – which now stretched right across the valley floor – was still some fifty metres away from the gates.

Inside the area 'guarded' by the huge gates, I could just make out a lush sylvan setting, with young trees arched over a pool being fed from a small waterfall. The gatekeeper beckoned an aged cripple at the front of the procession, who shuffled forwards holding the hand of a child. The gatekeeper took the man's crutch, set it against one of the gateposts and gestured for the old man and the boy to walk into the cool of the welcoming clearing.

The column of marchers was moving once more, now animated by two lines of black Balaclava-clad Hamas fighters. Flanked by white-coated Médecins Sans Frontières medics in bloodstained gowns, they were triumphantly carrying a banner, bearing a quotation from Revelations.

Swinging my binoculars left to check out the procession's newest followers I was surprised to come across a small European party. Proudly at its head was a group of girls I instantly recognised as 'The Salford Trio': Alice and Elsie, between them holding the hands of little six-year-old Bebe, all still dressed in their Taylor Swift celebration party outfits. Then came Shane Warne, in his distinctive baggy white flannels and green Australian cricket blazer, holding the hand of Mandy Rice-Davies, followed by a slow-moving chauffeur-driven Mercedes coupé with a serene Princess Grace sitting quietly in the back. Behind the Merc came two members of the Fab Four: John Lennon, dressed in a vivid yellow three-quarter-length frock coat, and George Harrison wearing a stylish crimson coat and carrying a matching tricorn hat. Then came Freddie Mercury, in his signature black leotard, arm-in-arm with George Michael. Following them was the unlikely sight of two of Britain's most notorious tax dodgers: Knotty Ash's Ken Dodd leading a sleek black stallion ridden by Lester Piggott. Towards the rear of this sombre but good-natured procession, which tailed away down the valley all the way to the beach, was a neatly-turned-out group of youths in army battledress, wearing helmets bearing the blue and yellow colours of Ukraine. They were followed by two donkeys, each laden with huge straw baskets of wine corks. I recognised the two dark-skinned Syrian viticulturists leading them as being from Lebanon's famed wine-growing Beqaa Valley. Bringing up the rear was the lonely uniformed profile of Field Marshall Erwin Rommel, 'The Desert Fox'.

The sun had reached its zenith. I flipped my baseball hat around to cover my neck and drank the last of my water. Rolling up my anorak to form a pillow, I lay my head down to snatch 40 winks before my descent to the beach. When I awoke it was dusk. Through my binoculars I could just make out the foamy trail left by the last departing ferry boat. I swept the field glasses round in a horizontal arc to scrutinise the valley floor. From side to side it was utterly deserted, with no sign or remnants of the huge procession I'd watched. Nor was there any trace of those great silver gates or the gatekeeper.

19

Di's Welsh Diner

ANY hope that Ricki might have had for a lie-in that morning was rudely shattered by a violent fracas on the landing opposite his bedsitting room.

The Indian girl who sold the *The Big Issue* outside the Post Office all week was unceremoniously ejecting her boyfriend, complete with all his belongings. After her final torrent of abuse, the door was slammed shut, though this didn't deter him from trying to reopen it with his boot.

"What's up then?" Bleary-eyed, unshaven and dressed only in grubby grey boxers, Ricki menacingly filled the frame of his own doorway, hands on hips.

"Piss off!"

"You what?" He was across the landing in a trice, grabbing a handful of the youth's black goth T-shirt. "She said she doesn't want you in there. So scarper!" Then he wheeled round and hurled the fellow horizontally across the landing as if shifting a sack of potatoes. The youth crashed into the newel post of the staircase, winded.

Ricki scooped up the sundry belongings - shoes, coat, and a cardboard box full of CDs and tapes - and flung them angrily down the stairwell to the landing below. "Right. Now you can either follow that lot by walking down the stairs on your own two feet. Or I'll help you down. Head first. What's it to be?"

There was a morose silence from the landing floor for a full half-minute. Then the youth grudgingly got to his feet, silently collected his belongings and made for the stairs, yelling a farewell "Stupid twat!" once he'd reached the safety of the floor below.

"Tosser!" was Ricki's response.

Ricki's dishevelled neighbour nodded her gratitude and retreated into her flat. He returned to his own room just as his phone rang.

"Rick? Hi, it's Mel. How y'doing boyo?"

"Oh hi Mel. Fine, fine. Just been doing some light removals here. Where are you?"

"I'm at Clearance Sid's. I tried to reach you yesterday evening, but you must've been out."

"Yeah, the bingo went on a bit late. S'matter of fact, I wanted a word. What time are you finishing at Sid's?"

"Oh I can get away any time; it's very quiet today. He's out collecting. Listen, I had this really upsetting session in one of my internet chat rooms yesterday. I need to talk to someone about it. Couldn't come over, could you?"

"Give me half-an-hour, will you, Mel? I'll grab a coffee on the way, then maybe we could take a drive out of town?"

"Why – where we going, Rick?" his friend asked plaintively.

"You know that lay-by you're always going on about?'

"You mean for my Diner?'

"That's it. Hey, why not show it to me this morning? I've heard so much about it and... well, there's this business offer that might come up, see? I figured you might be interested."

Unhesitatingly came the reply: "If you say it's OK, Rick, sure. Can you pick us up at Sid's then?"

"I'll be over shortly, mate."

Ricki decided to snatch a hasty breakfast in the only coffee bar in the town which dispensed decent coffee: Ascari's. It was only two minutes' walk from his lodgings and so he grabbed a quick breakfast there most mornings. The corner shop was brightly lit and welcoming from within, with the original terrazzo doorstep - emblazoned with a big scripted A - already washed down and gleaming clean.

Founded by a Welsh-Italian who'd emigrated to the town from Cardiff, it was now run by Marco, his grandson. Though now in his 60s, he was still a fine figure of a man, solid without an ounce of flab.

"Morning Ricki. Usual double espresso, is it?" He didn't look up from pulling and pushing the levers of the hissing Pavoni espresso machine.

"And a chocolate croissant please, Marco."

In his heyday, Marco had been an outstanding road-racing cyclist. Many said that with dedication, he might even have made the grade to the Tour de France. Consequently, the interior of Ascari's was a veritable shrine to the heroes of cycling. The café's walls were lined with dramatic black-and-white action photos of all the cycling greats: Anquetil, Induraín, Merckx, Pentani, Ullrich, Coppi, Zabel. Pride of place was reserved for Tom Simpson and the famous picture of him on his fatal ascent of Mont Ventoux. Marco and Simpson were born in the same year.

Ricki walked across to a bar stool at the window and began studying the *Socialist Review* he'd brought with him. A minute or two later Marco brought his order across. "Bit early for you isn't it, Ricki?"

"Couldn't sleep, mate. Anyway, I'm on my way over to pick up Mel."

"And how is old misery-guts Mel? Barmy as ever?" Marco laid the plate and coffee cup in front of Ricki and stared aimlessly out of the café's big window at the traffic, wiping his hands on the crisp white towel tucked under his apron belt.

"Listen, the bloke's just a bit disturbed, that's all. He's certainly not barmy."

Marco turned and walked back to the bar. "I reckon anyone who can carry a torch for an old strumpet like Diana for seven years has got to be a bit touched." Then shrugging: "Still, he's your mate."

Ricki didn't bother to respond. He finished his breakfast and left to pick up his van. Marco was serving an office worker and they merely exchanged nods as he walked out.

He drove across to the jaded wasteland where Clearance Sid's second-hand furniture emporium - ironically called *Cornucopia* - was located.

The warehouse was sandwiched between an abandoned, graffiti-decorated multi-storey car park -- once the pride of the local council - and a car breakers' yard. The half-opened galvanised shutter door retained the optimum level of gloom in which Sid pulled off all his best sales. Shabby, unfashionable, worm-ridden furniture was literally stacked to the roof trusses. Of course, there were bargains to be had - but Sid had already had all of them, slipping them into the real antiques chain well before the rest of the van load reached *Cornucopia*. It was unlikely *Flog It* would ever be filmed in Sid's emporium.

Sid had begun his career as a 'knocker', before graduating to whole house-loads of under-valued furniture. His reputation as the greatest house clearance man in south Wales was legendary throughout the antiques trade. All the best tales of old ladies being parted from Chippendale commodes and of Turners being found at the back of old wardrobes emanated from Sid's warehouse. Ricki often reflected that the name of the business had been cleverly selected not to indicate bargains (which is what the poor, benighted customers imagined) but to mark what a horn of plenty it had been over the years for its disreputable owner. Mel had been Sid's part-time warehouseman, tea boy, verbal punch bag and general dogsbody for nearly two years. It was the first job he'd had since he lost his job at the steel mills. Being by nature a troglodyte, Mel found *Cornucopia*'s semi-hermitical ambience ideal.

When the blue van rounded the corner of the side street, Ricki spotted Mel slumped forlornly in an old uncut moquette armchair, its springs and webbing leaking onto the pavement. He was reading an astrology magazine. His demeanour seemed to self-ignite as he caught sight of his best friend. He was slightly built, almost frail. Though barely in his 40s, his light gold hair was severely thinned. He wore a paint-stained green quilted body warmer over a Llanelli rugby shirt, bleached crumpled jeans and severely scuffed Doc Martens.

He jumped up out of the chair and pulled the big shutter down, clamping a giant combination padlock through the hasp on the pavement.

Ricki greeted him through an opened window of the parked van. "Hi there, Mel! Jump in, mate. Now what's been getting you down?"

Mel made several attempts at slamming the passenger door shut until Ricki leaned across and grabbed the pull strap. He started the engine and they took off.

Mel stared through the windscreen in silence for some minutes, as if analysing the question.

"It's this Diana chat room I visit, see? Last night there was this French bloke on. Said there was a story in the current issue of something called *Le Canard* about some missing forensic report, which showed - listen to this Rick - which showed that there were abnormally high levels of carbon monoxide in all the three bodies that they pulled out of the wreckage in the road tunnel. Abnormally high, Rick! So what d'you make of that?"

Ricki negotiated the last roundabout before they joined the main road north to Cwmbran, then relaxed his grip on the steering wheel a little. "Well, of course, *Le Canard* is a notorious scandal sheet, Mel – it's the French equivalent of *Private Eye*, but even more libellous. I'd take anything they print with a large pinch of salt, mate. So why'd they reckon this report's gone missing, then?"

"S'obvious, innit?" Now in full 'conspiracy mode', Mel swung round to glare disparagingly at the driver. "MI6 has got hold of it! Dodi's Dad's always maintained that British security was behind the whole thing. So, I reckon that this confirms it, don't you?"

"Confirms what?"

"Why, that they'd modified the exhaust system on the Merc, so that fumes were fed into the car of course!" Mel was now becoming quite agitated (and Ricki wasn't paying full attention). "By the time they were in the Alma tunnel the air conditioning was pumping a lethal gas into the car's compartment, causing poor old Henri Paul to behave erratically. Stands to reason. Bastards!" He flung his magazine on the floor.

"And that's what you've been so upset about?"

"Yeah. I tell you, I didn't get a wink of sleep last night worrying about it."

The road was getting more scenic now, and Ricki hoped that his friend might start to calm down. "Well, I'm sorry I wasn't around mate. Fact is, I was being propositioned by a lady. Well, a woman, actually. A woman police constable. Ex. I think you know her. Sian Jones? Remember her at my trial?"

"Oh yes, the brunette. It was her bloody testimony that really did for you, wasn't it, Rick?"

"Well, yes, I suppose you could say it just about put the tin lid on it for yours truly. By the way, she's blonde now. Says it's natural."

"You don't say. Get a chance to check?"

Ricki grinned. "'Fraid not. Another time, p'raps."

"So what did she want?" Mel's interest temporarily overshadowed his Di-depression.

"Dunno. She was pretty schtum about what was involved. Just said a geezer she knew had been asking her if she knew of a couple of blokes who'd be up for some sort of special assignment."

"What sort of special assignment, Rick?"

"Search me, mate. But I shouldn't imagine it's rare brass rubbing."

"More likely to be something dodgy, would you say?"

Ricki stared ahead through the windscreen pursed his lips. "Almost certainly."

After a pause Mel came back with: "Would that be *very* dodgy? Or just a bit iffy?"

"Mmm. More likely to be in the 'very dodgy' category, I'd say, Mel." The driver turned briefly to look at his passenger. "How'd you feel about that, mate?"

"Me? I've got no problem with that, Rick. After all, I've done fencing, haven't I?" He gazed out on the passenger's side at the valley vistas which were opening up.

"No, Mel, what you do *isn't* fencing, mate. It's just re-selling gear that the crafty old bastard you work for has blagged off innocent old ladies. That's not fencing." Chastened, his friend fell silent, burying himself in his astrology magazine, *The Tower*.

Ricki's van struggled to cope with the big climbs which were now coming up as they headed along the scenic section of the Heads of the Valley motorway. Now the distant skyline was decorated by rows of slowly rotating wind turbines, looking like children's paper windmills. Mel remained glued to his magazine.

Then Ricki caught sight of a second batch of 50 or more disfiguring turbines, all gyrating in slow- motion. "Hey, did you know that there are turbine spotters now, Mel? Just like those anoraks who used to stand on the end of the platform at Cardiff Station. Remember them?" Still no response. They drove on in a brooding silence. "Listen mate – I shouldn't get too upset about that French pillock last night. The internet's full of headbangers." He wondered whether this universal condemnation probably included Mel.

Mel glanced sideways through the passenger window. "Did I ever tell you I went to see that clairvoyant – the old biddy who sits in the lobby of the Old Market? The Upper Dock Street entrance?"

"Yeah, I know who you mean. Looks a bit like Vera Lynn."

"More like Vera Lynn's Gran, I'd say."

"No, you never told me, Mel."

"She read her cards for me."

"Oh yes? About Diana?"

"Princess Diana, Rick. Yeah. After she'd passed over."

"And what did the cards say?"

"Said her wedding to Charles was a marriage-made-in-Hell."

"Really? Why's that?"

"Stands to reason, when you think about it, doesn't it?"

"Explain it to me?"

"A Cancer and a Scorp!" Mel snapped. "It's got disaster written all over it, hasn't it?"

As Ricki regarded astrology about as plausible as UFOs, he decided to tread warily. "I suppose there could be something in it. What was Dodi?"

"Aries."

"Well, there you go!"

"Exactly. Different kettle of fish altogether, innit?"

Mel's black mood seemed to have passed. He pulled himself up from his slumped posture and looked eagerly through the windscreen, tucking the copy of *The Tower* into the glove compartment. "It's coming up on the left, my lay-by. Just after the brow of the next hill. You'd better slow down and indicate left."

"Don't panic. I think I know where it is."

Immediately after the crest, an enormous tree-lined lay-by was revealed on their nearside, running parallel to the carriageway. Now in use only for the temporary storage of road-mending materials, it was all of 300 metres long, with wide entrances at either end. A small mountain of fly-tipped refrigerators was the solitary occupant of this redundant road which predated the motorway.

By the time they had pulled off the road, Mel had regained some of his animation. The view westwards across a low farm hedge was breathtaking. The crystal-clear visibility of the morning air offered a vista of several miles down the Gower Peninsula and a widescreen view of fields, hills and distant mountain ranges. Above, was a spectacular Rubenesque cloud formation. A solitary glider from the Black Mountains Gliding Club could be seen moving silently from one cluster of cotton wool to the next.

Ricki parked midway along the lay-by and the two friends climbed out. "Flamin' Ada, Mel - you never said anything about the view!"

"Not bad, eh?" Mel had regained his self-confidence. "And look at the length of this strip, will you? I reckon you could easily fit four of Eddie Stobart's artics in here, nose-to-tail. And still have room for some cars and vans. What do you think, Rick?"

"Easily. So what are you going to do for your tea shack then?"

"Diner! D'you mind?" Mel replied indignantly. "This is going to be a really classy mobile unit, I tell you. Nothing like those tacky sheds and caravans you see on most lay-bys."

"No rubbish!" said Ricki in his best Max Miller cockney voice. "But what about the pillocks from planning? Those superannuated jobsworths down on Cathays Park? You'd never get permission to build something up here in a million years!"

Mel looked around, adopting a superior air like a landed gent in a Turner landscape.

"But I'm not *going* to be building, see? I'll base it on one of them American 1960s Airstream caravans - the ones with all that beautiful corrugated metal cladding on - you know the kind? Rock musicians use them on tours. Sid reckons he knows a bloke in Cardiff who could ship one over from the States for me cheap. I'll tow it up here every morning behind an old Land Rover and take it away each night."

"Seems you've got it all worked out, old son."

"Pretty much. One or two small details to finalise."

"Like finance?"

Mel paused to glance at the disappearing glider. "Well, yeah. Like finance."

"D'you suppose Sid might help out?"

"Sid? No way! He'll throw a major wobbly when he knows I'm quitting."

Mel sailed on regardless, as if funding such an outlandish enterprise was the least of his problems.

"On the far end of the Airstream, I'm going to have a long silver mesh sleeve – a bit like a wind sock – mounted on this stainless steel pole, look. Probably be about two metres long."

"I know - for the Welsh flag to fly on?"

"Prat! 'Course not. It's to simulate one of Princess Diana's slinky silver stockings. The ones she wore under that famous off-the-shoulder black velvet 'Revenge' dress. Remember: the night after Charles snuck off with old Prune Face to that railway siding? I'm going to call it 'Diana's Diner'." It seemed there was no detail too small to escape this conspiracy theorist.

"And do truckers have a big thing about Diana?"

"Princess Di? Is the Pope a Catholic? They most certainly do, mate! I've done quite a bit of research into the subject."

Ricki smiled to himself. "I thought somehow you might've."

"Do you know how many Diana websites there are on the internet?"

"No, not off hand. But I'm sure you're going to tell me."

"Only 1,300 worldwide, that's all! And there are more than 100 dedicated chat rooms. Pod Casts too. Admittedly some of them are used by out-and-out nutters, but in the ones that I visit who do you think are the most frequent visitors?"

"Gay estate agents?"

"Long-distance lorry drivers, that's who!"

"That's remarkable!" Ricki tried to sound gob-smacked, but he was having a job keeping a straight face. The solitary glider banked sharply and headed back to Talgarth.

The two friends silently walked back along the length of the lay-by. Mel seemed slightly apprehensive - still seeking Ricki's approval. He nervously studied him sideways-on – like a little dog - as they approached the van.

Ricki was checking the volume of heavy lorries speeding by. "You're going to need a couple of really eye-catching signs half way up both hills, so they'll slow down in good time, won't you? A life-sized cut-out of her dressed as a waitress, perhaps? And staff. Are you planning to hire Di lookalikes?'

"Natch. I want you to help me write some job descriptions. I'll drop 'em in at the Job Centre in town. And I want to get a listing in something called the *Egon Ronay Guide*. D'you suppose Marco at Ascari's knows him?"

"I doubt it, but I'll ask."

As they arrived back at the parked van Ricki turned to face his friend. "Listen mate – I think you've done a remarkable job thus far. It's a great spot. Really, I mean it! Truly. It can't fail!" His pal gave a broad grin and nodded, delighted by his mentor's affirmation. "Now we've just got the small problem of finance to organise for you. Guess I'd better make a date to take Sian Jones out for a Chinese."

They climbed back into Ricki's van to head south down the motorway. An unspoken bond had somehow been made between them: they'd become partners and it was now up to Ricki to come up with a financial master plan which would keep this improbable dream parked safely in its lay-by.

Mel simultaneously slammed his passenger door and switched on the car's radio. Booming Motown bass notes filled the interior. "Hey shush Rick – it's the Supremes!"

Ricki had long ago decided that his friend's attention span could be measured with a micrometre.

20

Gaudí

THE letter lying on the doormat was the one he'd been anxiously anticipating. Carrying the embossed silver word MATRIX in one corner and a Swiss air mail postage stamp in the other, it was a response to a suggestion he had emailed to the Editor of the prestigious arts monthly. His writings as an architectural journalist had taken a nasty dip in the previous six months and a major illustrated feature in what was widely recognised as providing the best architectural coverage globally, would give him the 'leg up' he (and his bank manager) craved.

The subject he had put forward was the long-anticipated completion of Barcelona's Basilica of the Sagrada Família, the culmination of the greatest work of Antonio Gaudí. First commissioned in 1882 by loyal devotees of The Order of St Joseph, this epic architectural creation was consecrated by Pope Benedict in 2010, after several interruptions by wars – civil and European. Now there was talk of a further commemoration by the new Pope Leo XIV. The Swiss Editor's courteous response was enthusiastic, stating a firm copy deadline, and he set to with gusto to make travel and accommodation bookings.

He opted for a small boutique b&b off Las Ramblas. It was within walking distance of La Sagrada and close by the legendary Palau Güell, which Gaudí had built for the wealthy industrialist Eusebi Güell and was now ranked as a World Heritage Site by UNESCO. He only had time to make a lightening tour – absorbing much of the great architect's unique style in its interiors – before heading for the cathedral. Gaudí's treatment of the Güell mansion's exterior, such as rooftops and chimneys, would often be whimsical and extempore. Once, when putting the finishing touches to Palau Güell, he was chastised by the local authority for standing in the street and directing tilers to try out different types of ceramic finishes to the chimney pots. Such detail, the bureaucrats insisted, must be shown on the architect's drawings, not shouted from the street!

Parque Güell, another of the maestro's projects for the same client, was a revolutionary urban development on the edge of the city, ambitiously planned as a self-contained workers' township. It was also a flattering 'nod' to the emerging English garden city movement, richly overlaid with Gaudí's polychromatic inventiveness. The 12-hectare park had lakes, terraces (where the architect's 'signature' serpentine benches lined with broken blue and white ceramic tiles first appeared) and a grotto-like market hall for Saturday fruit and vegetable traders. The death of Gaudí's wealthiest client prevented its completion and it was eventually bought by Barcelona's city authority and turned into an urban park.

Queues of tourists were already forming to join conducted tours of the nearly complete cathedral, but his signed letter from the Editor of *Matrix* gave him privileged admission to a VIP entrance gate, where he was greeted by a hard-hatted female architectural student who was to be his guide.

"We're incredibly busy today," she told him in faultless English. "I'm afraid I can only spare you one hour. So, what would you like to see first – for your article?"

"Would it be possible to go up one of the towers?"

"*Ciertamente, senor*," she said, adding with a smile, "so long as you don't mind the stairs. There's no lift!"

"Fine by me," he replied nervously, not realising the Alpine-like ascent he'd agreed to. "And when we come back down, after I've studied the models and maquettes, I like to inspect the maestro's designs of decorative ironwork, which I've heard a lot about."

"*Hierro forjado*?" she replied. "Fine. I'll direct you to one of the side chapels after we've descended."

Handing him a hard hat she led the way to the base of one of the four huge sentinel-like towers which flanked the cathedral's main entrance. Ghostly white plaster figures were occasionally randomly set in small niches in the main towers – as if being carried aloft on some celestial chair lift - simulating figures of the deceased on their way to Heaven. One, a Roman legionary, was said to have been modelled on a waiter in a café Gaudí patronised.

In an increasingly narrow space – only lit by small porthole-type windows – they ascended just over 200 steep steps, with the vertical stone walls increasingly encroaching into their space, so that his shoulders were now brushing against the stonework. "Only 20 more steps, senor," his guide reassured him from behind, "then we will arrive at the crossing bridge."

Through one of the portholes he could see that fragments of a deep red glass had been inset into the tower's masonry walls. "Murano glass from Venice, senor," the young guide told him, seeing him spot the distinctive ruby red discs. "It will last longer than the maestro's usual ceramic decorations."

Whether the great Catalan architect had intended it this way – his unswerving devotion was never doubted – for the English writer it certainly felt like climbing to Heaven! Virtually all of the Basilica's 18 slender towers were visible during the ascent.

The promised 'crossing bridge' was indeed mind-blowing. The stone stairs ended abruptly at a short stone-paved bridge-link, which stretched out into space (over 150 metres above the cathedral's entranceway), with wide porthole windows facing out and down for those brave enough to look! Then a careful one-step-at-a-time descent.

The visitor's guide could see that he was speechless – half from exhaustion, half from sheer vertiginous fright. She clutched him gently by the arm. "Terra firma, senor – and your chance to meditate on the maestro's unique understanding of the 'plastic' qualities of iron! It was a late skill he refined from working on the restoration of Palma de Majorca's Cathedral, you know. You won't be disappointed, I assure you!" Then touching the peak of her hard hat she hurried away to her next VIP appointment.

The journalist moved across the central apse towards a side chapel, to avoid the veritable tsunami of visitors who were now arriving. On a good week in summer, he had learned, it was not unusual for more than 90,000 tourists to pass through the turnstiles (Barça would love numbers like that). Multi-lingual signs with such warnings as 'Two hours wait from this point' were often helpfully displayed along the pavements.

The altar rails in the empty chapel were swung open, indicating that Mass had recently been said. The inner ribs of one of the towers were decorated with a chequerboard of gilded ceramic pieces, which glowed gently, reflecting the ruby light cast by the Chancel lamp. But it was the construction of the metallic framework beneath the altar rails which was so unconventional: matt black matching coiled steel springs. It seemed there was no decorative medium that Gaudí had not embraced and mastered.

As he made his way to the main exit gates, the writer glanced back. Working from rope-slung cradles, he saw that painters had begun the delicate task of gilding the internal curves of the cathedral's four great central towers. In the early stages of construction these had all been formed from dressed Montjuïc stone, but the city quarry's stock was exhausted by the mid-1950s and later towers were formed from cast concrete. Used for many of the city's great buildings since Roman times, the durable sandstone's grey-green colouring had always held a special fascination for the Spanish architect.

The English visitor headed away from the crowds in search of a quiet bar. He would take a late snack lunch, gather his thoughts and make some notes of his initial impressions. Up the hill was a pavement café with a good vantage point. He took an outside seat and ordered a ham *bocadillo* and a San Miguel. From here the majestic solemnity of the towers, lit by angled sunshine, was truly awe-inspiring.

As he tucked into his sandwich and jotted some notes, the writer recalled the final hours before the great architect's death. It seems he had made it a daily dawn 'devotion' to view his masterwork from just such a vantage point. And on this particular day, he was taking in the panorama not from the pavement but standing in the deserted street. Around the corner came an early-morning tram, hitting him a ferocious glancing blow and striking him unconscious onto the cobbled highway, where he lay in a pool of blood. Passers-by mistook the old man's dishevelled appearance for that of a homeless vagrant and walked on. It was a sympathetic shopkeeper who finally summoned a horse-drawn ambulance and by mid-morning Gaudí's close friends were at his bedside at the *Antic Hospital de la Santa Creu* for the poor, where he died without regaining consciousness, a few weeks short of his 74th birthday.

The writer closed his notebook, sighed and reflected: 'Can beatification be far away?'